ENERGY FIX

WE DON'T LIKE YOUR KIND AT VRS.

The characters and events in this book are fictitious.
Any similarity to real persons, living or dead, is
coincidental and not intended by the author.

Chapter 1

Linemen for Advance Cable Maintenance Equipment Company (ACME) began their days before sunrise. Joe Fitzgerald leaned in, kissed his wife on the forehead, and headed out for his day in the dark hours before daybreak. He made this a ritual and schooled countless journeymen over his twenty-plus years on the job to "expect the unexpected."

He traveled the twenty minute commute into Gardenville, and reflected on his good fortune. Somehow he'd managed to land his sorry butt with an angel of the purest kind, quite the chef as well. As the savory aroma wafted inside the cab he was reminded that she made the best split pea soup this side of the Mississippi.

First man in, Joe removed the industrial padlock from the yard gate. He swung both sides open wide for business, and drove his personal vehicle around the back of building three.

He parked in his usual space, hopped down from the bench seat, and opened the rear access door to grab his Igloo. *Gosh, I love that woman to death.*

4 a.m. and still dark, he used the glow from the truck interior light to be sure he held the right key. His

boots crunched across the gravel lot to the warehouse door.

Joe slid the gold master key into the keyhole, and leaned his weight into the thick metal door. His eyes took a moment to adjust to the pitch black darkness. He reached for the bank of light switches and BOOM! A loud electrical explosion blasted his body.

He perished in an instant.

The surge burst his lunch box. Olive green pea soup splattered alongside his dead body resembled algae atop a pond.

Death by electrocution is barbaric.

Henry Ashcroft arrived at the same door thirty minutes later. His right hand extended, he made contact with the knob. Two thousand volts of energy seared end to end through his body, and exited his left foot. Fortunately the voltage path missed his heart.

The force rocketed him across the parking lot where he landed on a pile of wood pallets.

Chapter 2

Dead asleep in her youngest daughter's bed, Fiona heard the faint sound of her alarm. Disoriented, she quietly rolled off the side of the bed and tiptoed across the hall to silence the thing. The cell phone displayed 4:45 a.m. Her brain ached. *No one in their right mind gets up this early.*

I'll start with the lunches and a coffee so I don't kill myself sleep-showering.

She skulked down carpeted steps, then gasped as her feet hit the cold kitchen tile floor. *Slippers Fi.*

Fiona drew her Starbucks latte from the fridge and plopped it into the microwave. She pushed express cook, two minutes. *Crap, take the lid off ya fool.* She yanked open the door and removed it. Condensation dripped onto her bare toes. "Fudge!"

She reached for a paper towel and the entire roll fell from its cheap plastic under-the-counter gripper. She packed two *Lunchables* into brown paper bags and wrote quick notes. "Love you, Mom." Crappy nutrition, but a treat today. The girls would be delighted.

Fiona knew she needed to organize better for future lunches. Getting out of the house by 5:30 every morning was going to be challenge enough.

Last night, to prepare for this too-early morning, she'd stopped by Kroger to get the girls something easy to pack for their lunches. To her delight, James Leon, a dear, old friend, had also happened to stop for a few necessities. Their conversations always covered more than greetings. Yes, his wife was fine. Yes, he missed her working at the warehouse. Yes, he was delighted she'd gotten this job. He'd seemed a bit distracted, and claimed he really needed to run.

"From me?" She batted her eyes at him in mock seduction.

She felt better when he laughed before he went on his way.

As she stood under the hot water, her thoughts drifted to the meeting Victoria'd scheduled out at the warehouse a year or so earlier. For the last two years she had simply been an hourly consultant to a company owned by Victoria's father; Various Reliable Services (VRS). She worked on her own schedule from home or the office, depended upon the project. She loved the friendships she'd developed.

She especially enjoyed partying with Vic, one of her newfound best friends. Working for Vic's father could be lucrative. Benefits to boot.

In fact, her getting the work in the first place came through a high school pal, Rex Alden, and his consulting firm. He wasn't pleased that the contract work would be ending, now that Fiona had received an employment offer at VRS. His firm made big money farming her out forty to fifty hours per week via ACME, James' company.

In a way, she breached an unwritten code of conduct by working for ACME's associate. She might have felt bad about it, except they paid their staff a fraction of what they collected, considering them their cash cows. There were rumors flying around about a new rule that VRS would no longer allow contractors like Rex Alden's firm. She guessed pressure from a couple of others still in the field with both ACME and VRS required him to grin and bear it.

Maybe she should feel a bit more like a traitor after all.

One day about a month earlier, Victoria Jacob made the deciding call to her father. Before Fiona could even consider the situation fully, he offered big money to place her on the VRS staff as a social media specialist. No interview, huge money, basically the same or less hours with a guaranteed salary and benefits. How could she turn it down?

Mom is more excited than anyone that the girls and I will finally receive benefits. That was how Fiona justified her final decision.

Fiona had loved the casual atmosphere at the warehouse where she'd worked for the past year. The linesmen and employees of ACME were all so chill, and appreciative of her graphic and web projects. She had only been to VRS HQ twice, both times intensely creeped out by the high security guard gate, fencing, and door keys

She shuddered, suddenly cold in the hot shower. *Getting a real job is chilling.*

She stepped out of the shower to grab for a towel and noticed her pale white complexion in the mirror. A look up and down her body exhibited no sign of summer tan lines, and ten plus pounds of winter extra. *Lordy, let my black slacks button and zip this morning.*

The changes in store for her daughters bothered her, too. A single mother, self-employed for their entire life, Fi was always available on a moment's notice for field trips, forgotten gym shoes, or lunches. Driving to VRS early mornings and arriving home late evenings was going to cause some commotion.

Sure, Allison was 15 and Lauren 13, officially old enough to get themselves ready, and finally both in the same school so they could walk together. What are the chances they could get along well enough to get it done?

She also anticipated turmoil from within her new company over how she got the job in the first place. Recently she had introduced Victoria to her pal Kyle Spencer. Now, officially engaged, the happily-ever-after event was set for September. Rumors flew that the job, "created out of thin air," repaid the local matchmaker. She hoped that her graphic and web skills would squelch them. In the meantime, she guessed she just might need to tough it out for a while.

Out of the shower, the fact of rising before five for a six o'clock start time still grated on her. Driving into downtown Detroit made it worse. As she checked her wardrobe, she realized the date: St. Patrick's Day. That meant something green.

It's a Tuesday at least. Monday would have been even more awkward.

As Fiona pulled out of her neighborhood on North Campus in Ann Arbor, she experienced the collegiate demonstration of green beers and loud music. *U of M is a tough school academically, would it not concur that the students would be smart?* Fiona pondered the logic in setting one's alarm for drinking. *Please let this be a phase that is out by the time my girls hit university.*

She laughed aloud at the fact that, since her 40th birthday, she had started quite a bit of this talking to herself. *A sure sign of old age.*

Her cell rang. Although it was an unknown number, the 248 area code indicated the VRS headquarters prefix. *Better pick up.*

"This is Fiona." She waited a moment, but heard nothing.

Still on side streets, she vowed not to answer once on the freeway headed out of town. She briefly mourned her tennis coach's wife who was killed by a distracted driver a few years ago on M14 between Ann Arbor and Livonia. Even this early, the morning commute could be a truly deadly stretch.

She hung up. The phone began to ring again almost immediately. She depressed the green key on the phone, then switched into speaker mode. She said nothing.

"Hey, girl, is that you?"

"Hello?" The voice rang no bells. She paused and pulled over before the entrance ramp to the freeway. "This is Fiona."

"Hey, girl, it's me, Ebony, your new boss. Or sidekick, whatever." She heard a woman's chit-chatty voice chirp through the speaker. "Just making sure you're heading my way right now. This place is already filling up."

Fi glanced at the digital display: 5:23. *Who in their right mind is up and at 'em, perky and upbeat at this hour?* "Yup, on my way."

"Okay, girl. Make it snappy. I am gonna wait out here and save you a parking spot so you'll know where to go. And not have to walk into the lion's den all by your lonesome."

Jeez, syrupy sweet. Egad. "Gotcha. My GPS says I'm 36 minutes out, don't freeze to death waiting on me. I can find my way in." Fiona figured the woman dreaded her arrival. Why sugar coat it?

"Nah, I'm right here waiting on your ass. See you in a few."

"On board." The phone clicked off before Fi could respond with her usual affirmative. *Well, shit, the Garmin now says 39 minutes.* Fi huffed. *I'm gonna have to make tracks. Unbelievable to have a 6 a.m. start time on day one. FML*

She made a quick lane change to head east when the phone pinged a text message. *No texting while driving,* she reminded herself as she depressed the screen to open the message. The speedometer read 80 mph.

"There's a man I want to show you. Also be careful. A ton of police lurk around the club here, so take it easy. Don't rush. I got my heat on!" The message included a smiley face emoji.

Fi quickly typed back "k," keeping one eye on the road.

Oh, my freaking gosh, she's gonna show me a man? Not introduce me? Not "I got a guy I want you to meet?" This day already feels like a long one. I should still be warm in my bed asleep right now.

As she pulled off the Fisher freeway with a chain of vehicles all headed to the same place, the clock read 5:58, and traffic crawled. *Well, shit, late on my first day. How nice.* As she made the turn onto

Madison, she saw a woman jumping in place, probably trying to keep warm. As she pulled closer she slid down the passenger side window.

Fiona was immediately taken aback with how beautiful this woman was. Combination Halle Berry skin, Michelle Obama stature and attire. Her overcoat tied with an elegant ribbon like the Inauguration one pictured online. Green gloved hands that could have been stolen from FLOTUS' closet. *And she runs the entire marketing department for this group?*

"Ebony? Sorry I'm late." Fi's heart filled with dread. Her pasty white reflection in the side mirror desperately needed sun.

Ebony looked at her phone. "6 a.m. sharp, sister. Pull in right here. Let's go."

Okay, above and beyond, thought Fiona. *Saving me a spot out in all this?*

"Thanks a million. That was one hell of a line to get in the driveway up there."

"Listen, girl, we're heading in through the back. Did you know this is a 'gentlemen's only' club? They do allow women in for parties and whatnot. Follow me."

Ebony made no mention of the nearly 40-minute wait that followed. For that, Fi gave a quiet thanks, vowing to play nice from this moment forward.

They climbed a set of stone stairs that led to a back door. Fi noticed radio and television vans parked in the back lot.

"I suppose this is big news, green beer and a few ladies at the male only club," she remarked, cigar smoke wafting out as Ebony pulled the door open. *Ugh, but chin up. At least I didn't need to circle for a spot. Play nice, Fi.* She almost laughed aloud. *Oh boy, talking to myself again.*

Ebony didn't reply, just put her hand out for Fiona's coat.

As the two women entered the room, a dozen or more overweight, middle-aged men turned to check out the wares. "Ew, ew, ew." Fiona's thoughts accidentally got audible.

"You'll get used to it." Ebony's voice held a curt edge as she strode toward the food table. "Let's get some carbs in you before I treat you to the Irish coffee."

A long banquet table loaded down with a continental breakfast sprawled along the back wall, supported by omelet stations at each end. Fully stocked and tended bars stood on each side of the make-shift radio booth on stage. Tons of people chatted and sipped on green refreshments.

Fiona helped herself to a nutty sweet roll.

Her eyes immediately caught on her pal James bad-tempered beside the stage. He argued with a tall guy. Fiona's senses kicked into high alert. She'd worked side by side with him in stressful situations and heated meetings. Never did he ever lose his cool.

The tall guy looked rich, every inch of him. From his perfectly styled hair, unseasonably deep tan, down to his Italian shoes. Even his silk tie looked Italian. It boasted a deep emerald green shamrock pattern, flawless for the occasion. James appeared less than pleased with this man.

"Who's James talking to?" She grabbed Ebony by the elbow and pointed.

"One, it's rude to point. Two, James is being talked at. Three, you'd better get one thing straight about the big boss." Ebony paused to swat Fiona's hand off her arm. "Reed Jacob, the big guy, only talks. He's got no time for listening. Sure as hell, you do not say one word to that man."

With that, Ebony strode away. Fiona stood alone in contemplation of the lethal tenor.

Chapter 3

So, what was James doing here?

Fiona edged closer to James and her new boss who was "talking at" him. *Curiosity killed the cat*, she reminded herself, to no avail. Her pal looked like he was in trouble, which was enough for Fi.

"For Christ's sake, Reed," James was saying. "It's the IRS, not one of your cronies we can pay off."

James' raised voice turned a couple of heads besides Fiona's toward them, but he paid no attention. He waved a letter at Reed.

"Captain James." Reed's voice dripped with sarcasm.

"The IRS doesn't scare me any more than my wife does. They crank out letters like that one designed to frighten gullible people. They insist we fill out all kinds of ridiculous forms, but it's just to keep themselves employed. A man in your position should know that. You also should know that we have an entire floor of finance and accounting reps to deal with letters like this one."

Reed took the letter from James and surveyed it a moment. "Why in sam hell did they send this to *you*?"

Not waiting for a response, he crumpled it into a ball and shot a basket in to a trash receptacle.

James flew after the paper to retrieve it.

"I honestly believe you think you're above the damned laws of this country, Reed," he said as he returned. "Last thing I want is to see you in jail for something like this." His voice raised another notch. "Do you even know what you put me and my guys through? Damn it all, you get this to Audrey at headquarters, Reed, and tell Donavon to weigh in as well."

Reed chuckled. "You really think mixing accounting and legal is a good idea, James? You're dumber than I thought." He wiped a bead of sweat from his brow.

The room isn't that warm, Fiona noted. *Is his humor an act to disguise worry?*

"Go fuck yourself." James pocketed the letter and glared at Reed.

"Ahh, not necessary to fuck myself, friend." Reed widened his big white grin for one of the models on stage with the radio crew. "Not at all necessary today. This here's a party." His eyes drifted to a blonde now, who returned his stare with a come-hither look. Still eye-locked with the blonde, he said, "James, fetch me a Jameson, and a champagne for the lady, won't you?"

"I mean it, Reed." He made no move to play waiter.

"Reed, James, don't look so serious!" JT Morton, the radio host, peered at them from atop the four-step stage. "Peek, drink, and get Mary!"

JT pulled the blonde to the edge of the stage. "Come up here, gentlemen. Let me introduce you two to Mary."

He gestured for a waiter backstage to bring the tray full of champagne glasses he carried to join them also.

Fiona noted that although James climbed onto the stage, he did so with reluctance.

Reed took two glasses and gracefully handed one to the blonde. "A toast," he said. "To mutually beneficial relationships!"

"Agreed!" JT held his glass up high.

"Whatever." He ignored the tray of champagne. "Lighten up. This isn't the time for squabbling, boys."

James just glared at him.

"While I get Reed to welcome our guests, tell Mary an Irish story, will you?"

Instead, James walked to the side of the stage where the blonde joined him. He left Reed with JT.

"So, Mary, what do you do for a living?"

"Oh. My name's not Mary." She giggled and snuggled her free arm under James' elbow.

He sighed.

Fiona watched as JT pulled up a mic.

Reed joined him, but the blonde and the champagne retreated backstage.

"Ladies and gentlemen, welcome to those of you here in the mock studio, and our listeners at home on your AM dials. May I introduce you to the man responsible for supporting our live broadcast this morning?"

JT Morton motioned to Reed, handing him another microphone. "I'll quickly remind our listeners out there that Sir Jacob is owner and chief do-gooder at VRS and ACME. Both companies are hugely important employers in this community. So please give a warm round of applause, or hold your green beers high. My friend and our corporate sponsor of the day, Reed Jacob!"

The room exploded with clapping and cheers.

As JT backed away to join James, Reed took center stage, waiting for the noise to silence. He needed to clear his throat twice before anyone would let him speak.

"VRS is committed to community involvement extending way beyond our energy corridors. We pride ourselves on being active in the community, working closely with stakeholders, and you, the customer, to ensure our energy services meet specific needs. We also support events such as this fine morning with you, JT Morton." He paused to wave toward JT and James.

Applause followed. Reed waited patiently for it to diminish.

"I love a community that works as a team to provide reliable energy, while giving back. This is why I invested my life savings in VRS, and entrusted ACME to my best friend James Leon."

Reed motioned for James to come to his side. "This man runs the maintenance arm of our system. Trust us to remain loyal to our community for many years. Now, join us in tossing back a green beer in honor of our host JT Morton, guys and dolls. Three cheers for a long-lasting mutual partnership!"

Fiona noticed that although he smiled, he didn't look happy.

# # #

With a sigh of relief, James cleared himself from the stage. *Reed did like to make a show.*

His cell pinged from his pocket with a text. He read the dire message with alarm, then made a beeline for the door.

"Hey, hi there." Fiona caught him before he reached it.

"Oh, hey. Yeah, hi." James realized, with his mind still on Reed's recent behavior, his distraction showed. "Sorry, Fi. How the hell are you?" He smiled and pulled her in for a hug.

"I know you warned me about this shindig and all, but, wow, I had no idea of all the pomp and…"

"Oh, this is all bullshit, kid. Once you get into headquarters and get to the real job, you'll be hating me for recommending you."

"Hate you? Gosh, James, never in my life have I ever met such a cool and courageous gentleman. I mean it. You are Robert Redford with a bit of Daddy Warbucks, all rolled into the most supportive and generous man I've ever met. Not kidding. My mother is over the moon that I finally get pension and benefits. You know, a real job. I can't ever thank you enough, James."

"Your mother raised one smart cookie. You tell her I said so. Listen, I gotta run. Seems something's up at the shop. Damn, if I can take one single morning off! You know how it is out there."

"Honestly, James, I'm going to miss heading out to the warehouse daily. Call anytime I can do something for you guys. And let's book lunch soon. With Veronica and Martha. I miss them already."

He knew employment at the warehouse with the maintenance crew had been a great gig for her. He made sure she was paid consulting fees on top of the retainer fee Rex's firm paid her. With his help, things looked up for Fiona and her daughters financially. She needed benefits, which she didn't have while self-employed.

"I'll have Vee book us up early next week, kid. Good to see ya. And congrats on the job. I am real happy for ya."

She gave him a sideways look that meant she wanted to believe him, but realized something was a bit off. *Hell, we are all a bit off, drinking at six a.m.*

Chapter 4

James hustled toward the exit when he felt a pull than a push. Manhandled into a dark enclosure, the hand over his mouth smelled familiar.

"Listen asshole, I cannot have you causing a scene out in public places, do you hear me?"

"Reed?" James was taken aback at the rage.

"Who the fuck do you think you are showing up at a party with some legal bullshit? Don't you know that I made you? I own you. You were a bullshit power line supervisor when I pulled you up out of the field, you dick."

"What the hell is this?" James broke free of the grip Reed had on him and felt around for a light switch. Nothing. "Shit, man, what the hell is going on here? Why are you coming down on me? I'm trying to save you from yourself, for cryin' out loud."

"What will help me right now is you keeping your trap shut." Reed pulled on a chain hanging down from the ceiling and illuminated the fact that they were in a cleaning closet. Bleach and buckets, shelves of supplies crammed the space around them. "You fucking say one word to anyone about sponsoring, or money, or whatever the fuck, and I swear I will…"

"I think you're losing it, man. I really do." James was trying to use a calming and concerned tone.

"Are you hard of hearing? I mean it. You are stepping your feet in a big steaming pile of horse shit. You are supposed to be thanking me, licking my ass if I ask you to. Not hassling me on the details." Reed was drunk.

"Okay. Listen. It's on me. I'm sorry Reed, I really am." *I gotta get to the shop.* "But we really do have something going on out at Falbrook. I got like six texts. Can we grab a drink after work tonight? I really am sorry."

"You'd better be. Fuck'n A, if I'm going to have a bunch of asshole auditors crawling up my ass because you can't keep your damned mouth shut."

"Not another word, boss." James backed to the door. "I mean it, not another word out of me. You're the boss. I'm just going to get the hell back out to the warehouse and keep the energy flowing, man."

"That's right. Keep it flowing. Until I say it doesn't, you hear me?"

James believed the man was definitely losing it. The two had history. *Shits getting real.*

Now he really needed to get to the warehouse. Surely, in all the excitement, the text misinterpreted events. "Joe is gone," he had read. Joe wouldn't leave, not without telling him first, but something was up. Something serious. Texts continued to ping on his phone.

James' frustration made him barely able to hold the steering wheel as he pulled out of the club and headed toward the freeway. He tried to call Jeanie on speed dial, but she wasn't picking up.

Probably for the best, he decided. She didn't need any more updates about how stressed out he was these days. Both he and Jeanie were eligible for AARP and should be sipping margaritas at their Florida condo by now.

This is on me. He scolded himself for falling into this trap with Reed.

Sure, he appreciated the cool million Reed had enticed him with as an incentive not to retire just yet. Yes, he was pumped to be named head honcho of ACME way back when. Damn it, though, he resented the fact that Reed truly had him over a barrel. ACME was to have been his. The IRS had contacted him because his name was on the books as president.

Reed initially agreed to stay on his own side of the fence with VRS. *Freaking various alright.*

That had certainly changed. Reed seemed to be getting drunker by the day, more erratic in his behavior, and James could feel something ugly coming his way. The IRS letter might just be the tip of the iceberg.

As he pulled his truck into the warehouse parking lot thirty minutes later, his heart rate soared. Fire rescue vehicles and ambulances blocked his path.

Lights spun atop, crews scrambled around them. *Holy hell.*

James slammed the truck into park. He jumped out and sprinted toward the building. He traversed around emergency vehicles and was met head on by his assistant Veronica.

She collapsed in his arms, hysterical. "Joe, its Joe. He's gone."

Her text had said as much, without all the drama. No mention of emergency services.

"Gone where, doll?" He couldn't shake the dark dread that edged toward him.

The ambulance crew seemed less in a hurry than he expected. Two EMS personnel packed up around Building One, while another loaded a cot with a black zipped bag. *Someone died? Why hadn't Joe called him? Why leave it up to Veronica?*

As they rolled past, James held Veronica. Head buried deep in James' shoulder, her body convulsed with sobs. She mumbled something about his head lineman, Joe Fitzgerald, words rendered inaudible by sobs.

They stood outside the center building, Building Two. He needed to get through the crowd into Building One. Through the window of the main conference room, James noticed several uniformed police officers, and a couple of suits talking with his foreman and a small crew of linesmen. Rather than try to pry Veronica off him, he buoyed her toward the back door of Building One. He needed to get her to his office into a chair.

Damn, it's Tuesday and Martha only works Wednesday and Thursday. Who can I call to deal with Veronica?

As James approached his office, he observed a group dispersed inside. Some uniforms, some suits. Cabinets and drawers lay open and disheveled.

"Can I help you, officers?"

Veronica still glued to his body, he situated her into a chair. Two men wearing dark suits pillaged James' desk with gloved hands.

"Is this your office, sir?" A uniformed police officer pulled out a small notebook, pen ready.

"Yes. James. James Leon, ACME president."

The officer wrote it down, then slid the pad into his shirt pocket. He moved in on James and Veronica, impeding view.

"You need to back up on out of here until we clear the room, sir. Take the lady with you, please. We have reason to believe there could be more unknown power surges or explosive devices somewhere in the building. Nothing is firm yet. We just want to be one hundred percent sure before you fire up any electronic devices and that sort of thing." As he spoke, the officer's arms resembled a crossing guard, one pointed as the other waved.

James stared at him, utterly confused. "What the hell is going on?"

"Sir, I am going to need you to cooperate." The officer took a more forceful stance, and eased his right hand to his holster.

"Okay. Okay." James did not like the look on that face. "Veronica, let's head out to my truck." It took finesse to move her to her feet. She seemed unable to respond.

He'd gotten her hoisted, and virtually carried her back through the building when Aubrey stepped in to help.

"Let me take her, boss, the cops want to ask you a few questions." James paused.

No one moved. Aubrey spoke again. "We're all heading to Tim Horton's across the way once cops clear us."

"Clear what?" James felt a surge of anger. No one had informed him about the details of the incident. "Geez, could one of you not call me on the radio?"

"Sir, it has been almost three hours since any of us has been allowed to touch any electronic devices on account of…"

"On account of what?" It was about time someone told him what the hell had happened.

"Sir, Joe was the first man in this morning, and…well. Um. Why don't I get Veronica across the road while you get caught up with the cops?"

#

The information the police provided floored James.

Joe had arrived at the warehouse a little before 4:00 a.m. "Not unusual for him," James expressed to the officers. Joe used to joke that someday he would beat his boss to work, although he never did, until today.

Joe had unlocked the gate and hit a light switch in Building Three. An electrical surge from some unknown force field enveloped him. "Sir, I can tell you, he likely died instantaneously." That was of no comfort to James.

"The next guy got lucky. Surge sent him flyin' across the parking lot." The officer went on to explain that a second surge hit another one of his guys, Henry, as he grabbed a doorknob. The current ejected him twenty feet from the building onto a pile of scrap wood. He sustained electrical burns on his right hand and left foot. Although he lived, an ambulance took him to the hospital to assess the damage the electricity had done while traveling through his body.

Two men arriving a little before 5:00 found Henry unconscious and called 911. Emergency crews discovered Joe dead.

Most of the warehouse staff arrived at 6:00, surprised to see emergency vehicles. All received strict instructions not to approach any of the three buildings. Power to the entire city block had been cut off. The police confiscated cell phones and laptops.

Somehow, amidst the commotion, Veronica managed to get inside the office in Building One. She hit the lights and started coffee all without incident. The police claimed that a back-up generator to Building One provided the power. Luckily it was not rigged with whatever buzzed in Building Three.

Seeing the lights on, a firefighter ran inside to drag her out, scaring her half to death. He gave her news of Henry's injury and Joe's death. That was when she messaged James with her frantic text before they removed the cell from her.

By the time James arrived at 8:00, the building transformed as command center. Crews still checked all laptops, cell phones, CPUs and electrical outlets for a potential trigger unit or additional threat. They also removed James' cell from him.

#

James paced outside, beside himself. His mind raced. He had never intended to appear at Reed's ostentatious St. Patrick's Day party, and had told several people so, including Reed.

No one could have known I would stop to see Reed about the IRS letter in Detroit before the morning meeting at ACME.

His pacing slowed. *No one knew I wouldn't be there. Every morning, except this one, I've been the first one to arrive.* He didn't like where his mind took him. *Was that electrical charge meant for me?* His body quavered.

The past few years, in his heart, he knew his desire for a lucrative retirement had been misguided. He told himself often enough it was all "for the best," but he knew otherwise. If Joe's death was no accident, he was just as responsible as if he had killed the man himself.

He had gone into this with his eyes wide open. ACME provided maintenance services. Simple math: spend one dollar on improving energy flow in the region, earn one dollar and nine cents from Uncle Sam.

James got in his truck to drive to Joe and Lydia's. He needed to be the one to break the news to Lydia, not the police. This must be personal, not a uniformed cop. He wished he could call first to tell her to expect him, but not with his cell in police custody.

The drive time to Joe's place gave him time to align some recent suspicions.

Reed had taken very good care of James since their mutual departure from Midwest Gas & Electric five years earlier. The filth he felt over being on the take was easily washed away by thoughts of retirement in style.

It was all a scam, the take downs, fixing, rebuilding, and charging of some government entity. Plenty of people skimmed the government– white collar crimes – plus VRS owned plenty of blue collar boys in positions to take a fall if they were exposed. James knew the CFO at VRS had barely completed his GED. The CFO's gal was the economics wizard, when she wasn't on her knees under his desk.

Lately, spooky things had begun to happen. Lots of accidents. The changes Reed kept making were rapid and haphazardly planned, keeping folks off their game. They were spending too much, too fast, drawing unwanted attention to themselves, which was the reason, James believed, for the IRS letter.

But Reed's comment earlier upset him to his core: *I made you. You were a power line supervisor, now you own a big fancy schmancy utility maintenance company with unlimited funds. You should be thankful, not hassling me on the details.*

Reed was literally coming unglued.

James considered calling him about the accident, if that's what it was, and Joe's death as a result. As CEO, Reed had the right to know, but a reluctance born of worry prevented him.

Lay low, he told himself. *Maybe he already knows.* He examined that thought. How could Reed know if the first person Veronica called was James?

His next thought, the one that kept hovering in the background, caused him to swerve out of his lane and nearly sideswipe another vehicle.

Maybe Reed ordered the hit.

He shook the thought away, but it returned full force.

Holy cow, he was not at all pleased to see me this morning. Did he? Could he possibly? He knows. Shit. He ordered the kill. Dammitalltohell, Joe, why'd you have to be first one in today? I need you, man. Tears poured heavily, distorting his vision, causing him to slow down. He could have gone to the warehouse first, then swung over to the party. He hadn't needed to change his mind mid-traffic.

Impatient drivers roared past him, but James didn't care. Too many things began to add up. Reed had also been surprised to see him. The camaraderie that once existed between them no longer existed. Reed had begun dismissing James' authority and decisions. Lately, he had become far too active in taking over ACME, as if he planned for a vacancy.

Worse, this wasn't the first questionable incident at ACME. Two other people who voiced suspicions about billing approached James. He had encouraged them to confront Reed. The CEO would get to the bottom of any problems, he assured them. Both had met with accidents, too. One quit. The other one, still in the hospital, had indicated that he intended to quit.

When James pulled onto Joe and Lydia's street, he realized he was too late. The street already accommodated two police vehicles, forcing him to pull into their driveway.

As he exited the truck and climbed the stairs to the front porch of the bungalow, he heard some of the conversation.

"Did you know anyone who would want to harm your husband?" asked a strong male voice.

"No." Lydia's tear-filled voice and sobs as she bleated that one word broke his heart.

"Is there any reason to believe your husband was involved in any ill…?"

"Hold on here." James burst through the door. "This woman is in no condition…"

"Oh, my God. James." Lydia leaped from the couch and fell in his arms. "Tell me it isn't true."

Chapter 5

Once investigators finally released the ACME warehouses to get back to business, James spent most of his time there. He knew all too well about Ohio weather. The first week in April came as no surprise. It was 65 on Wednesday with a snowstorm on Thursday. Along with the crazy weather came plenty of work for the ACME crews. Lines broke down due to heavy ice loads. High winds blistered men's faces with frostbite when they journeyed into the frozen weather to fix the lines. Complete chaos reigned.

Everyone welcomed the heavy workload. ACME staffers were eager to get back, needing the beefed-up paychecks after nearly three weeks of absence. Investigators and fire safety crews seemed to have taken forever combing the three warehouses for evidence. The shut-down had affected each tight household budget in Falbrook. No one owned insurance for a plant closing.

James became so busy, he almost forgot that each morning he came in early he might be putting his life at risk. Besides, a man just couldn't live his life thinking the next moment might be his last. He had work to do.

He might have convinced himself that a danger no longer existed when a man walked into his office.

James recognized him from somewhere, but couldn't quite place it.

"Sorry to barge in on you like this," the man said. "I'm Detective Wright Danielson. I just hoped you would answer one more question for me."

Irritated with the interruption, James stood, tried to put on a pleasant face, and stood, holding out his hand. "Pleased to meet you."

Maybe the lie showed. Detective Danielson shook his hand, but he still wore an expression of apology.

"I know you want this whole thing to be over. So do I. More than you know. Although that investigation is closed, officially, some things just don't make any sense to me."

"What doesn't?" James knew several things that bothered him, but doubted the same things affected Danielson. For example, Danielson's office wasn't monitored. James no longer enjoyed the luxury of believing whatever happened in his office might escape Reed's notice.

"Well, ACME seems to be accident-prone. This was the third incident in less than two months. I'm wondering if they're connected. What do you think?"

What could he say, that people who asked questions faced trouble? He shook his head.

"More to the point, I recently discovered that you were always, until St. Patrick's Day, the first one into the office. Isn't that true?"

How had he learned that?

Not waiting for him to answer, the detective pressed forward. "I can't help but think that you were the intended victim, Mr. Leon. Have you considered that?"

Before he remembered to say nothing, his head betrayed him. He nodded. Joe's death still hurt like a son of a bitch. A wave of anger began to replace the fear he had almost squashed.

He met Wright Danielson's eyes straight on. Reed monitored everything at VRS, most likely here at ACME too. He took out a pen and wrote on the notebook at his desk. "You're barking up the wrong tree, Detective. The investigation is closed." He tore off the note and palmed it. "Good day," he said as he shook the detective's hand again, this time pressing the note into Danielson's hand.

"Very well, then," he said.

James Leon let out a sigh as the detective left his office.

Back in his car, Detective Danielson opened the note. It read: Reed is having a press conference tomorrow at 1 p.m. You never know just what you'll overhear.

Chapter 6

No one noticed Detective Wright Danielson who stood in plain clothes at the back of the media room. Out of his jurisdiction, being from Ann Arbor, but the case intrigued him. He found himself unable to let it go. Although he wanted to question James Leon more thoroughly, he appreciated the invitation to the press conference. Evidently James had his reasons for keeping silent.

Danielson wondered how Reed Jacob intended to explain the "accidental electrocution," as had been reported in the news. There was much more to the story, as evidenced by James Leon's surreptitious note.

He noted all three major news networks had set up television cameras. Reporters for radio, newspaper, and magazines filled the room. He pulled out a notebook as if he, too, were a reporter.

A tall, thin woman, hair pulled back by a clip, stepped up to face the audience. She wore a professional smile as she addressed the crowd.

"Welcome, everyone. My name is Fran Marner, press representative for VRS. The public face, so to speak." She laughed.

Polite chuckles followed.

"The accident that took Joseph Fitzgerald's life will impact us all for some time. Mr. Fitzgerald was well-liked by everyone who knew him." She paused.

"We are very grateful for all the agencies that came to our aid in Falbrook during this horrible accident. Emergency services on scene, police who kept order, and the investigating teams who literally combed through every inch of all three warehouses. Ensuring our people return to work, safely, is a top priority."

"Just this week, we re-opened our Falbrook warehouses. All investigating agencies provided us assurances that no wrongdoing, nor equipment malfunctions, caused the accidental electrocution of our beloved supervisor. Their conclusions cleared both VRS and ACME of any responsibility in the accidental death."

Lots of use of the word "accidental," Wright noted.

"We are all terribly sorry that this occurrence caused the accidental death of Joseph Fitzgerald. He will be sorely missed."

She paused as if in reflection, then turned toward a man striding toward her. A broad smile beamed from him.

"Now, let me introduce you to..." She gave a light laugh. "Most of you already know Reed Jacob, the founder and CEO of VRS and ACME companies. He feels a deep familial responsibility for all our employees and our safety, and would like to say a few words in closing this matter today."

Danielson chuckled under his breath. *I'm sure he would love this incident closed*, he thought.

"If you ask me, press conferences only complicate matters," he heard a woman behind him say.

"Equal opportunity press coverage," another woman added. "Any chance to parade in front of the cameras. He'll have a positive spin, you'll see."

The detective backed up a little so he could see the two women. Both were attractive, one just as dark as the other was light. Neither appeared to be impressed by their boss.

"I knew Joe," the blonde said. "To say he'll be missed just doesn't cover it. He left a great, gaping hole." She turned her attention to Reed Jacob.

"Mr. Jacob, you have the floor."

Reed adjusted the microphone to accommodate his towering frame. "Thank you all for coming today. And thank you to the greater Detroit community for the tremendous outpouring of support over the years. I want to personally assure everyone that VRS and ACME are committed to providing safe and lucrative jobs for citizens of the region. Getting our Falbrook employees back to work in a safe and secure workplace is of paramount importance to me and the rest of our headquarters staff. We applaud the professionals who were able to investigate and close the file on this accidental, unfortunate happenstance."

Accidental, unfortunate happenstance, Danielson wrote in his notebook, putting question marks after the words.

"VRS and ACME personnel have all been cleared in absolution from any further review. Our safety record is still the very best in the industry, and we will be adding more high paying jobs in the area within this calendar year. I invite everyone to check out our new and refined website for opportunities to join us as we continue to top the list of *Fortune* Magazine's Best Companies to work for. You want to work for a good company? Sure. A great company? Definitely. But work for VRS or ACME, the best damn companies in the greater Detroit area, well, that's a no-brainer." Reed paused as his eyes traveled over the crowd. "We offer generous bonuses, paid time off, parental leave, visionary management, and a sense of purpose as a community partner unmatched by any other. Come join us as we grow to become the preeminent best place to work of all time!" He started the clapping so others would follow.

They did, Danielson noted, with enthusiasm. Evidently Reed sold money as well as electricity.

"Yippee," the dark woman said, her voice dripping with sarcasm. "We're adding more staff."

"And you think that's a bad thing?' The blonde seemed surprised.

"We sit on our thumbs all day as it is. Remember when you met Ivan Gregory?"

"The one you call I-Greg? Barely. I never see him."

"He's one of our bosses. And, he's a prime example of a person working at a job who never works. What does he do all day? Who knows? Does he care that his secretary, Marci, wrote a romance on company time? He might care if he had any work to give her. But since she looks busy, and he has no work to give her, well, the money comes in, and the money goes out. I know you know what's up."

What was up? The detective poised his pen to take more notes.

"I have my suspicions," the blonde said slowly. "A dollar nine for every dollar spent, is the rumor I heard."

A dollar nine from where, Danielson wanted to know.

"Truth."

The detective watched as reporters left, knowing he ought to follow suit, but his curiosity delayed him. When he noticed that the two women started to dismantle the set-up, he stepped in front of the blonde.

"Here," he said as he took the podium from her. "Let me take that. Where does it go? I'm Wright, by the way."

She smiled at him. "Fiona," she said. "This is my boss, Ebony."

Ebony gave him a broad grin as well. "Can't find too many gentlemen around here. My thanks goes double. Let me show you the storeroom. This should take no time at all now."

"So you two are the ones in charge of these sorts of things?"

"Sometimes. Usually Fran helps, but she needs to be somewhere else right now."

"Fran Marner, the PR person?"

"That's her. You a reporter?"

"No. Do you want these in there, too?" He pointed at a couple of chairs."

"No. Those stay." The blonde looked around at the room. "I think that does it," she said as she returned the mic to its place.

Wright followed with the mic stand, setting them beside several others in the storage area. "It was a pleasure meeting the two of you." He wanted to include both women, but his gaze fell on Fiona. She had a kind of quirky smile that he found intriguing.

"I couldn't help but overhear," he said. "Something about a dollar nine for every dollar spent."

Her face suddenly became unreadable. Wright realized he had just stepped over a line.

"Well, it was nice meeting you. If you think of anything extra, please give me a call." He handed her his card.

At least she pocketed it, he thought as he walked away, realizing he just might have blown his chance to find out more.

Chapter 7

Fiona headed back to her personal laptop to make a few notes. Reed had said something about new jobs. *Check the website to see if something has changed on the positions offered.*

To her surprise, the site didn't look any different from the day she applied. In fact, she found her own job and title as one of those being offered. Was Reed dissatisfied with her?

But as she checked further, she found that I-Greg's position, and his secretary's, were also listed, as well as Ebony's and a number of others where no vacancies existed. What was this? Why offer jobs that were already filled?

Or was it as Ebony insisted, that jobs were offered for the sake of getting back one dollar nine from the government for every dollar spent?

"You gonna spend all day in there?" Ebony stood in the doorway, hands on her hips. "Those eggs aren't going to stuff themselves."

"The Easter Egg Hunt! I completely forgot!"

"Well, this is one day we have something to do, so let's get to it!" She led Fiona into a smaller conference room where Fran had already begun to unload boxes of cheap, tiny toys that she piled in the center of the table.

"Assembly line," she said with a grin. "You get the plastic eggs started over there." She pointed to one end of the table where opened boxes revealed hundreds of artificial eggs.

She then shoved a smaller metal box at Ebony, gesturing for her to be at the end of the line. Empty boxes waited for filled eggs to be deposited.

When Ebony opened the box, she found it filled with twenty dollar bills. "For the love of..."

"Reed wants all the eggs to also have one of these."

"Shit." Ebony glared at the money in the box. "Twenty dollars an egg? I want to hunt some. Kids these days should be happy with quarters or silver coins, not twenties."

"I think Martha over at ACME said she has over a thousand dollars for us to stuff," Fran said. "Even the candy eggs should have at least a dollar. Crazy, right?"

Fiona gave both women a guilty look. "My stupid idea," she muttered. "I remembered being at the ACME warehouse and seeing all the candy-stuffed eggs, wishing they at least held a dollar. Shoulda kept my mouth shut."

Ebony laughed. "So that was how all this got started. What'd you do, go to Reed personally?"

"Actually, she told me," Fran said. "Someone must have heard us speaking. Let's get it going, girls."

"What I actually suggested," Fiona said as she opened eggs for Fran to fill, "was that maybe we could cross-promote with other companies, offer discount coupons from local eateries and such, and that the occasional dollar might be a nice bonus. Kids love to get money."

"By the time it got back to me," Fran said, stuffing eggs with toys and sliding them toward Ebony for their twenty dollar bill, "Reed said he loved the idea of controlling what went into the eggs. No coupons, just small toys and cold hard cash. 'The kids will love it,' he insisted. He's a money man, after all."

He sure was, Fiona thought at the end of the day, stretching the kinks out of her back.

# # #

James watched the annual Easter Egg Hunt, the children hunting in glee once the first twenty dollar bill was found. Reed was in attendance, a smug smile on his face. "Cold hard cash," he'd heard Reed murmur. He guessed nothing got in the way of Reed and cash.

A nippy breeze stirred their clothing. The state park near ACME's new warehouse, not far from the metro airport, provided few trees to break the wind. *The children didn't seem to mind*, James thought as he drew his jacket closer. Maybe it was the bite of the wind, but it looked like the crew and their families appeared to be a bit on edge. He edged toward a group who spoke in a huddle. Although he kept his eyes on the children, he focused his ears on the group's conversation.

"Joe basically took the bullet for James," one person said before his wife shushed him, seeing James.

He glanced at her and moved on. While the children happily gathered goodies, the adults collected in pods of gossip. The main topic centered on the series of accidents, especially Joe's.

Some things are not fixable, James thought. He had accepted the resignations of several warehouse workers. The money was great, especially with the recent bonuses, but the sense of unease prevailed.

True, everyone was back to work. Things appeared normal on the surface. But investigators still performed occasional visits, and environmental agencies sent their people as well. The media also sent the occasional reporter who tried to dig into their lives.

Maybe people knew a kind of monitoring had invaded them, as well as those at VRS. When people spoke, they kept their voices hushed.

Then there were all the new forms. The tiniest incident reports needed to be logged and reviewed over and over. Hell, the odd splinter required an incident form. Although he toured the warehouses and kept things running, James stayed out of the office as much as possible, taking his paperwork home. And he arrived much later in the day.

This morning, though, he sat beside Henry, who was still hospitalized with severe burns.

"Sheesh," Henry exploded when he heard about all the forms. "We provide power and energy, for cripes sake. Why all the fuss?"

"I guess they're covering all bases, doing whatever possible to avoid another death." A slow sigh escaped him. "Joe was best man in my wedding, Henry. I'm not going to lie. I miss that bugger more than I can tell ya. How are you feeling?"

James had not slept much in the month since the incident, making it his personal mission to be more present, and responsible, for all of his guys. He had his suspicions, as did just about everyone else, but kept his personal opinions close to the vest when he spoke with his employees. Only his wife Jeannie knew the belief that ate him up inside: Reed wanted him gone.

James explained to Henry that Reed had re-opened the warehouse after he received the report from investigators that it was all just an accident. James was still trying to convince himself of that, but his gut told him otherwise. He asked a trusted few to keep digging for any signs of wiring out of whack, broken circuits, secret passageways, anything to explain the surge of electricity powerful enough to kill someone.

"I'm doing better'n I have a right to," Henry said. "You say even though the investigators left, the safety crews are still on site?"

"Yep."

"Good ol' Reed, taking care of us like that. Let him know I'll be making a full recovery soon. It's great to work for a company who watches out for us the way he does."

Ignorance is bliss, James thought as he drove away from the hospital. *No sense in disturbing such a gracious soul.*

Inside the safety of his truck, the one place he knew wasn't monitored, he called Jeannie, the only one he trusted to talk things out with.

When James initially presented the idea that Reed wanted him dead, Jeannie poo-pooed the idea.

"That's crazy thinking," she said. "He chose you specifically. If he wanted you so much, why would he try to get rid of you now?"

"Because I challenge him. I don't know what he's got going, but something's very wrong." Then he told her of other incidents where people had questioned Reed about inconsistencies and billing issues. "They either get hurt, or they quit." *Or both,* he'd added silently.

Although Jeannie said nothing at the time, she came back to him later with a tale.

"You may be right," she said in that slow, thoughtful way he loved so much. "You remember our dinner last Wednesday with the Jacobs? Reed was his usual loud, boisterous self, overshadowing Tulie, like he always did. I could see something bothered her, so when she suggested going to the ladies' room, I went with her."

James used to like their regular Wednesday dinners. Years ago, Reed had insisted on it, saying that since Tulie had no friends, and that Jeannie was a comfortable person to get to know, they needed to get together each week. Besides, it might prevent her from nagging him to include her in every outing he conducted around business.

After the incident, the invitations ceased. Last Wednesday was their first in over a month.

"Golly, it's good to see you, Jeannie," Tulie had begun. "Reed told me you and James had decided to cut out and retire to your place in Florida about a month ago. I told him we'd have to get a place closer to you all in Naples if that was the case, because you're my only friend who understands how this industry can involve some long hours for the guys. It's not just doctor's wives these days." Her laughter held an edge of desperate relief.

"Retire?" The statement caught Jeannie off-guard. She laughed too. "Imagine James retiring. That's such a funny thought."

"Well, regardless, I'm glad you're not. It's lonely at the top." She chuckled at her own joke.

The thought of James retiring kept her giggling all evening. That, and maybe the wine. It wasn't until later that night when it hit her. *Reed* told Tulie we were moving.

When she put it together with another odd occurrence, she became alarmed.

Zimmerman's Deli in Ann Arbor delivered a food basket to the Leon's' condo in Naples the day after Joe's death. With all the commotion of heading up north for the funeral, and helping Lydia with arrangements, she'd simply tossed the box into her pantry, forgetting all about it, until the following Thursday.

By then, everything fresh had spoiled. She tossed most of it, and this time read the enclosed note: "I will miss our Wednesday dinners. Love, Tulie and Reed."

"She said 'I'." Jeannie showed the note to James once she realized he was right. "This clearly indicates she acted alone. Reed had nothing to do with her gift box."

He nodded. "Joe died on a Tuesday morning. Reed didn't text me on that Tuesday or Wednesday, the way he always did to confirm our standing appointment. Check my phone." He pushed it into Jeannie's hands.

"Honey, I believe you." She passed it back. "I finally believe you."

But James pressed forward. He called up his phone log to confirm that neither Reed nor Tulie had made contact on the Tuesday nor Wednesday about cancelling the dinner.

"Furthermore," James continued, "Reed Jacob claimed to have known nothing of the incident until the next day—Wednesday. Why was there no confirmation text on the Tuesday verifying where and when to meet for dinner? Reed always chooses. He always texts. It's always the first text I receive on Tuesdays, always at five. But that morning I received nothing from him, which I thought very strange since he is so OCD with planning and scheduling."

"What now?" Jeannie was near tears. These had been a long few weeks, zipping up and back to comfort and console Lydia. "I am literally exhausted by the whole deal James, just quit. I beg of you, just quit."

"Maybe you don't understand the magnitude of the situation here, Jeannie. My guys are my life." Jeannie shot him a mean and nasty look. "You know what I mean."

That day, they began to develop their exit strategy, one that included a way to keep the remaining employees, like Henry, safe.

To lighten the mood, James flipped on the stereo receiver and took Jeannie in his arms. On the radio he heard, "Anywhere you go, I'll follow you down, follow you down but not that far." It seemed apropos for a moment like this.

Chapter 8

The next morning, completely unaware of the drama surrounding their workplace, Fiona tried to convince Ebony, using the whiteboard in a conference room on the third floor, to understand their website issues.

She covered one entire side of the board with a picture of a window labeled "template." The other side contained line items including Twitter, Online Chat Room, Constant Comment, and Electronic Communication.

"The site we have is a sham. It needs to be pulled down and completely overhauled."

Ebony just frowned at her.

"You know what perplexes me the most? We have an in-house tech team of nearly two dozen people, yet we "farmed out" the website to the tune of fifty thousand dollars. It makes no sense to waste resources like this."

"You know what perplexes me? Who talks like that, Fiona? You're giving me a headache."

Fiona stared at her in surprise. "If you'll just listen a bit longer. We could have a site worth its weight. It could be a gold mine for those interested in our company."

"Look, you big geek, it's not that I don't understand what you have in that noggin of yours, but not once has the company ever talked about social media, website enhancement, and communication with customers or engaging in any internet platforms."

"Platform, eh? You want to talk about the fact that there is literally no freaking way your tech guys approved messaging with this thing? The infrastructure elements alone arc remedial. You could use Gmail and have more security communicating with this."

"Stop." Her voice was becoming shrill. "Just stop talking. VRS built their reputation on spending marketing dollars on community support and sponsorships, not by upgrading websites."

"Oh, yes, I know. I know that you all just throw parties and fund politicians who keep the deals flowing." She blinked at her own words. *Wait a minute, Fiona. Be careful. A dollar nine for every dollar spent. Remember?*

But it didn't sit well with her. They could have a company she felt honored to serve. This sham of a business caused her to feel dirty. Her heart longed to be proud of her work.

She met Ebony's hostile stare, unable to hold her own. Instead, she decided to try another route. "Why is it you all have what you call a company with no formal marketing plan?"

But instead of swaying Ebony to her side, the woman fumed as if barely able to hold her temper. She looked at the ceiling fixture, then at the walls. "Let's go."

When Fiona started to grab her things, Ebony shook her head and held the door open for her, wearing a no-nonsense glare. "Now!"

To Fiona's surprise, Ebony opened a janitorial closet and shoved her inside. She flicked on the light switch and closed the door.

"The walls have ears, you idiot! People lose their jobs when Reed feels threatened. Your job doesn't entitle you to challenge everything. Nobody asked you to get all high and mighty on us. Tell Reed how the company should be run. We do our part in the area, we give dollars back to the people for marketing. It's not like we gotta convince anyone to buy energy, for shit's sake."

A dollar nine for every dollar spent, Fiona repeated to herself like a mantra. "The walls really do have ears?"

"And eyes. And don't you forget it. You being a naysayer makes me think of one of Oprah's line. Y'know, where she says all those casting stones feel threatened and feel as if you don't have any value, or some such shit."

"I wasn't trying to…"

Ebony didn't even pause. "I know my value. I know I don't need to shrink down to less around all that web talk. You sound just like Ben, all full of yourself like that. I don't need him, and I don't need you trying to shrink me. I gotta blossom into more me doing me."

"I was not trying to shrink you, Ebony. In fact, I asked you to listen to my presentation because I admire you."

Ebony lost her hard edge. "Maybe you're not like Ben."

"Who's Ben?"

"My ex." She paused. "My soon-to-be ex. He talks like that, like you just did, and for all his words, it doesn't get us anywhere. As far as I can tell, it's all talk. And I wasn't kidding about it all giving me a headache."

Fiona laughed. "I remember this one guy talking all FTP and SMTP way back when. I think he wanted those acronyms to intimidate me. Web geeks are simpletons."

"Simpletons? They sound smart."

"They spend all dang day putting linear code into some cockamamie shit to make the internet work."

"Simpletons." Ebony started giggling.

"What I'm trying to tell you is that you all paid more than fifty thousand dollars for a bullshit template and no functionality whatsoever. Not YOU *per se*, but the company."

"Fifty thousand?"

"More than."

"A dollar nine for every dollar spent. Reed doesn't want the website to work, Fiona. He doesn't care. As long as he gets his nine cents for every dollar spent, he's just raking it in."

"What?"

"That little misadventure, in buying the services of a web developer that didn't know shit, just netted him $4500. What does he care whether it works or not if he's making money like that?"

But Fiona saw a bigger, more horrendous picture. She needed Eb on her side for this one. She leaned against a mop handle nestled in a bucket.

"All right. I got it, but what happens after VRS makes a boatload of money buying crap from some geek?"

"What do you mean?"

"Ya know, before I started working here, I made just enough money to support me and my two girls. Keep the lights on. Most of the time."

"Yeah? So? I'm there too, you know."

"Uh-huh. So are most folks I know. So, this is what really happens. For VRS to rake in all that dough, someone has to pay for it first. VRS charges a rate hike to the customer in the exact dollar amount that the know-nothing geek charged to develop the non-working website."

"What are you getting at?"

"Not only do we have a website that doesn't work, everyone has an increased energy bill to pay for it. I don't know if you can live with that, but I'm finding I can't. I worked too hard to make ends meet, and now I feel like I'm putting everyone else where I used to be. It's just not right, Eb."

Ebony stayed silent a while. Fiona could almost see her wrestling with the problem placed in front of her.

"But we do a lot of charity events…"

"Yes. You do a bang-up job on parades, public events, Little League sponsorships, and the like. But there's more to the picture. Do you have any idea about the politicians' pockets lined by this "startup" Reed created?"

"Startup," Ebony echoed. "We're on some very thin ice here, talking like this. Why don't we break for lunch?"

"Cripes, Ebony, lunch? We just had a coffee and donut an hour ago." This hadn't been where she had intended for this conversation to go. She could chow down with the best of them, but not at five meals a day.

"Fine, don't eat, but we're headed to Taco Bell before I have to listen to one more word."

Chapter 9

Fiona ordered an iced tea while she watched Ebony place an order for a meal.

When the food arrived, Eb barely picked at it.

"Start up," she said under her breath. "Simpleton. Who woulda thought?"

"What?"

"I need this job, Fi. I don't know how to survive without it. A few years ago, before I met Ben, I was doing all right. But he…"

She stared out the window.

Fiona said nothing, just sipped her tea and waited. Sometimes people just needed space before the words could come.

And then they did.

#

Ebony's alarm went off at 6:17 a.m. Not a big deal, she'd been lying there awake since about 4:37. As her son stirred in the bed next to her, she cursed herself for not turning the damn thing off when she initially woke.

"Back to sleep, sweetie. Momma's got an early day, but Ben will get you up and to the bus." She ran her hand across his forehead with love. Her impending break-up with Ben would surely upset his little heart.

Since his biological father had left before her son turned one, Ben had been the only father Skyler really knew. He had announced he would be leaving within the year. Bastard.

Bad enough to deal with his leaving as an adult, but children were always helpless victims in domestic matters. As she got ready for work, she wondered how to tell Skyler that Ben would be leaving.

Ben had, of course, done everything in his power to have Skyler at his side for basketball and football on the TV, playing the cool guy. It never seemed to bother him that chores or homework needed attending first. Winning the kid over had been how he had wormed his way into her life, Ebony discovered too late. Her son loved Ben almost immediately.

For a long time, she believed she loved him, too. The idea of living with a stay-at-home entrepreneur male father-figure in the home 24/7 sounded almost romantic.

Things never were what they seemed.

"When it's too good to be real, it's too good to be true," her mother often said. Ebony repeated the lesson once again, wishing she had listened to the advice years ago.

Ben had swooped in like a hawk within days of Skyler's father leaving them. She met him at a church mixer. Unemployed, working odd jobs fixing parishioners' computers, he had almost immediately offered to pick up slack on the home front. "Let me help you out, I love kids." The line worked.

Ebony held a high-pressure, relentless job as assistant to the president of VRS. Ben often arrived early and stayed to wait on the bus with Skyler. Often she'd return home to a hot pot of spaghetti or macaroni and cheese. When Skyler smiled ear to ear telling her how he and Ben had cooked dinner for mommy, her heart responded with what she believed was love. Eventually, she had allowed him to move in with them.

Thinking back, Ebony never recalled once seeing his place, which he had described as a "room without a view." More than likely he lived with his mother, she thought now, frowning. Not once had she met any of his friends or family, not even his proverbial mother.

Ben Carson, her potential knight in shining computer jargon, had been a puzzle from almost the beginning. While he appeared most helpful on one hand, he continually borrowed money from her. He explained that his start-up business needed a bit of capital to stay afloat, that once it got off the ground, they'd be swimming in affluence.

Her budget, when she'd bought the small house in Gardenville, was based on just her and her son. Adding a grown man, and his hobby-turned-start-up computer business, proved to be a huge financial drain. Although he promised time and time again to pay back loan after loan once the business really got going, it never happened.

To make business contacts, he bowled at a private Detroit club two nights a week and most Sundays. But he never seemed to have the money to pitch in for groceries.

After coming in from starting the car, she found Ben pouring water into the back of the coffee maker. "Hey," was all she could muster.

"Early one today, huh?" he inquired.

"Early enough. I was gonna make a quick cup of instant. You cool to get T up and to the bus by 7:30?"

She hated having to ask him for anything at this point. She was angry that he took over Skyler's room with his computers and random equipment, which relocated the young boy into her room. She wasn't about to have Ben sleeping with her, which she was sure he wanted.

Their paths rarely crossed of late. To tell the truth, she looked forward to the day she'd have more breathing room. He'd promised to be moved out "any day now." Then she could re-evaluate their dating relationship, from a more level-headed position. Living together was just too much.

"Yup, no problemo."

"Thanks." She hated when he did that random ethnic speak like he was a twelve-year-old boy responding to his mother about a chore.

The microwave dinged after the one-minute water heat up. She added a teaspoon of Columbian instant and headed for the door.

"You gonna be late this afternoon, too?" Ben asked.

"Nope." She turned back to face him. "In fact, I should be home early. I'd love it if you could not be here this afternoon." She and Skyler needed to talk about the situation without interruption.

#

"I never wanted you to be my assistant," she admitted to Fiona as she poked at her Taco Bell leftovers. "I didn't think I needed one." Then she raised her eyes, meeting Fiona's point blank. "You need to know what's at stake, girl. This is no joke. You gotta stop with all the complaining. I don't want to get into how important it is to keep your damn mouth shut, especially in the common areas like that conference room."

"On board," Fiona replied. Ebony hated that one, because she never was. But now she understood the reason better.

"But you're right. We need to find a way to do something. Even though I know not to challenge Reed directly, or to make waves by questioning where the money goes or how it's spent, we cannot stand by while illegitimate expenditures are racking up on our watch. Mouths shut all right, but asses covered."

"At least say nothing out loud while in the building."

"That especially."

"So why did you tell me your life story?"

"Ben isn't my life. I thought he was. Skyler thinks he is. I'm just tired of holding everything in. I'm not exactly asking for advice, but I needed someone to talk to. Bottom line, I wanted to explain why I just can't lose this job right now. If we do anything, we gotta find a way to expose Reed without losing everything I already worked for in my 401K."

"That may not be possible."

Don't I know it, she thought.

Chapter 10

Fiona and Ebony returned to utter chaos.

Fran met them as soon as they came onto the floor. "Where the hell were you two? Your boss—you remember him, the Vice President of Marketing?—found you gone, and…"

"You mean I-Greg? He actually left his office?" Fiona, who had no respect for him, grinned.

"You need to wipe that smile off your face right now. You were gone two hours, from what I understand. Reed wanted him to create a digital logo and print-out of the VRS and ACME logos, which was why he wanted you, Miss Smarty-pants."

Fiona clamped her mouth shut, upset with herself. The one time someone needed her for something important, she was trading stories with Ebony.

"I'll get to it right away," she said.

"That you will, right after you apologize to him and his secretary."

"Marci? Why?"

"She's in deep trouble because of you, Fi. She tried to contact you, but you must have your phone off, or something. So then…" She glared at Ebony. "…she tried to contact you to see if you could find her, with no better result."

She spun on her heel and marched away.

Ebony failed to keep her face expressionless. "I could lose my job for not doing it, rather than for not keeping silent," she muttered under her breath.

Fiona nodded. "Me too," she whispered back.

"Get to it, then come see me. We'll do a damage assessment." She hurried to her own office.

Fiona gingerly peeked into Marci's office, which fronted the VPs. He stood upright, shoulders back, hands on hips opposite her desk.

"Marci, you find out where the hell that new girl is yet? Reed wants to have some decals made for his Model T parade next month at the cruising event. We need to remind that bitch that at least one freaking person should always be available for requests coming in to the marketing department, for crying out loud. It's been two freaking hours!"

"Yes sir, right away, sir." Marci typed a text message to Fiona's personal phone.

When Fiona felt the buzz, she pulled it out. "CMI," she read. That was code for "call me immediately."

"Message sent, sir. Anything else?"

"Now that I'm thinking about it, order one of those magnetic boards like they have in other offices where people have to put a dot up when they'll be away from their desks. I cannot believe every time Reed calls I have to go searching for help."

Fiona saw him turn and enter his office. When she heard the door slam, she cringed. She'd really flubbed it this time.

"Yes sir, right away, sir." Marci spoke to his closed door, her face pale.

Fiona opened the door and walked in, ready to apologize.

"I heard Fran yelling at you outside the door. Don't bother to apologize, Fi. We're both in trouble."

"But it's my fault you are."

Marci frowned. "For not being here? Yes. But that's not all of it. I'll tell you about it later. I've sent you the specs of your assignment. You can get back with me tomorrow. Then I'll have that board he wants ready, complete with dots, and we can take a legitimate lunch together."

# # #

When they met for lunch at their favorite Mexican restaurant, Fiona noticed Marci had been crying. Fran stood beside her and handed her a tissue.

"I brought Ebony, too. That all right?" She felt awkward around so much emotion.

Marci shrugged her answer.

They managed to find a table in a remote corner, *lucky*, Fiona thought, wondering, besides food, what was on the menu this afternoon. It looked serious.

But no one spoke for a long time. They just ate in silence.

"I need help," Marci said finally. "I think I'm in trouble."

"Yes," Fiona said, wanting to apologize for putting Marci at risk.

"No, it's not you." She looked at Ebony. "As you know, because we have so little to do, I've been spending my time writing a romance novel. Besides, Ivan never seemed to care as long as I looked busy."

What a creative way to use up the empty hours, Fiona thought, impressed. She wished she had a talent like that.

"Well, Ivan knew more about what I did than I thought. I found out through Cruz, you know, the computer guy?"

They all knew Cruz. He was the one who kept the office computers running and the network functional.

"He told me that not only are the halls and the offices monitored, but so are the computers. He and Ivan are best buddies, I guess. But yesterday he stopped by my desk with a gleam in his eye, wanting… Oh, God, I hate this place! He said that since I put out for I-Greg sometimes, I could give him a little to keep my personal project a secret."

Fresh tears followed. Fran handed her another tissue.

"I found her in the ladies' room weeping her eyes out," Fran said. "She invited me to lunch with you two, saying we had much to discuss. It looks like we do."

"It wouldn't be so bad, but this morning Ivan cornered me at my desk wanting a little hanky-panky during office hours. How could I have ever found that creep attractive? We used to be an item. It was because of our relationship that I got this job here. He made me sick, and I told him so."

"Good for you," Ebony said, her lips pressed in a firm, no-nonsense line. "Same as I told Ben."

"Yeah, well, I was angry. I also told him that he was only hired for his ability to charm a crowd, that he had no expertise for the job he was hired to do, that I could do better, or maybe Fi could, and that his only contribution to this company was to give Reed his nine cents."

Fiona and Ebony looked at each other.

"He threatened to fire me on the spot, so I warned him he better not think of firing me, because I figured that some of the recent 'accidents' were probably due to people wanting to come clean, and that I had a lot to tell the police should he ever consider letting me go."

"Not smart," Fran said.

"No. It was the stupidest thing I could have done. He went to his office, and I ran into the ladies' room where Fran found me."

"I didn't know it was that serious," she said.

Marci looked miserable. "It's that serious," she said in a small voice. "I don't suppose there's a way out of this."

Suddenly all the girls were talking at once, trying to come up with solutions.

"Look at it this way," Fran finally said. "You just go back to work as if nothing happened, do your job, and we'll get together for another lunch tomorrow. Nothing will happen between now and then. I'm sure of it."

# # #

All three drove back in separate vehicles through the security gate. Names needed to be checked, comings and goings recorded at all times. Each one parked their car wherever they found room. It was a crowded parking garage, so Fiona found herself on the top floor. *No problem*, she thought. *The walk down will do me good. Or I could take the elevator.*

She decided against the elevator. All these meals out, donuts here, lunch there, an afternoon trip to the snack machine. The extra weight she'd put on nagged at her incessantly.

As she locked her car, she thought of Marci. A bit protective, she noted the secretary had parked on the level just below.

Fiona descended the first flight of stairs. There was a blood curdling scream followed by a thud. She nearly flew down the next set to the lower level.

She had almost rounded the corner when she saw Ivan enter the elevator on that floor. Heart thudding, she waited for the ding of the doors closing before peeking around the corner.

Marci lay crumpled halfway down the next flight of stairs, one heel caught in the metal mesh. Fiona witnessed some movement, she was alive, but definitely needed help.

Fiona's hands trembled and it took two tries to dial 911.

When she hung up with 911, she found the card Wright Danielson had given her. Her next call was to him. Not offering up any real reason, she asked him to meet her at Starbucks on State Street early the following morning. He agreed without inquiry.

Fiona waited for EMTs to load Marci onto a stretcher before she headed back into the building. They had spoken very little, aside from the "it'll be okay, we'll get through this together" type conversation. Both women knew full well they were being recorded if on VRS property.

When she met Danielson the next morning early, she explained how she had avoided Ivan since the incident. She had, in fact, seen nothing with her own eyes. Suspicions yes, facts, no.

During the meeting, Fiona's mother called. She talked around circumstances, eyes on Wright, as she explained away yet another calamity at her office.

"It was a terrible accident, they think. Marci always wore such high heels. Those stairwells are unforgiving, all metal railings and steps. I think she'll be all right, though. At least, that's what we were told." She ended the short call with, "I'll talk to you later, Mom." She hoped Wright understood the need to keep her family members calm.

When they departed Starbucks, a new resolve filled her heart. She needed out before something unfortunate sidelined her. Danielson had explained his being out of jurisdiction, his inability to provide any real protection, and then warned her to lay low.

She never would find out the truth of the incident. Marci never returned to VRS.

Chapter 11

Two weeks went by where the marketing trio simply avoided any talk of substance. They spoke about the weather, what shoe styles were coming back this spring; good morning and good afternoon the extent of their verbal communication.

But Fiona couldn't just let things lie.

"You've got more courage than brains," her mother told her once. Maybe it was true, but she needed some answers.

She boldly booked an outing for the three of them to visit the home office of ARDARK, the group responsible for creating the VRS website.

She used Outlook to schedule the appointment. The message simply read: "ARDARK outing."

"Ready?" Fiona and Fran approached Ebony's cubicle. Fi dangled her keys to signal that she'd drive.

"Ready!" Fran chirped.

"I'll meet you down there. At the lot exit ramp." For the last two weeks, Ebony had kept her distance from both Fran and her. Fi hadn't been sure she'd come at all.

"Great! See you in seven minutes, just outside the structure." Fiona realized she'd held her breath for a response in need of confirmation that Eb was on board.

It was a silent ten minute drive to the ARDARK Web Services offices. Fiona parked her Honda and waited a moment while Ebony reapplied gloss and exited the vehicle. Fran rearranged her skirt as she got out of the car.

"Good to go?" she asked, suddenly nervous.

"Go? We're here, you fool." Ebony scowled, but a grin pulled at one corner of her mouth.

Familiar with that almost-grin, Fran giggled.

Ebony's smile widened as she offered a small laugh.

"Yes. Here we are." Fiona was thankful for the lightened mood, but a ball of nerves fluttered in her stomach as they entered the building.

Try not to sound accusatory, she reminded herself. *Questions, yes. Accusations, no.*

The two were greeted by a young guy dressed in what looked like a prison jumpsuit. Even the receptionist behind the marble desk wore some sort of matching onesie that resembled a hazmat getup.

How odd, thought Fiona.

"What's with the pajama wear?" blurted Ebony.

"We have very important mainframe computers, housed in temperature-controlled environments here at ARDARK."

A valid enough excuse, as far as it went. Fiona was more interested in why they still used older mainframes in this day and age. But she chose to save that question for the principals they were scheduled to meet with. In this day and age, cloud based web storage and legitimate virtual private servers operated on much smaller CPUs. ARDARK seemed to have a dinosaur mainframe of some kind if it required protective outerwear to maintain it.

"Don't think for one second I am zipping into one of those jumpsuits." Ebony was on her game today, keeping Fran giggling.

"No, ma'am. You'll be meeting today in our conference room with, well… You'll be introduced." He hesitated just long enough for Fiona to turn and see his face. *A look of unease?*

"Right this way please, ladies," he said, recovering quickly.

This place and those get-ups are truly alerting my spidey-senses. What the heck is this place?

The group began the journey down a long, stark white corridor that led into a windowless maze of offices and workrooms. Fiona's body quaked with an involuntary tremor of alarm. In the silence she was sure she could hear the slow scrape of polypropylene covered feet behind each door. *If everyone in the building is wearing impervious coveralls, what might she, Fran and Ebony be exposed to?*

Fiona inched as close as possible to Ebony's ear and whispered, "Feel free to feign sick right about now, this place is giving me the heebie-jeebies something fierce."

Their guide stopped at an unmarked door and turned slightly to look them over. Nerves still jangling from the eerie scuffling sounds, Fiona felt the urge to turn back and get out. She almost heard a gigantic Big Ben-sized ticking in her chest.

The room was mostly bare except for a long stainless steel table and a dozen folding chairs neatly surrounding it. Centered on the table was an open case of bottled water and a tray of morning breakfast carbs: berry Danish, Croissants, and bagels, no cream cheese. The tray could easily have been day old but seemed untouched. The case of water bottles, on the other hand, clearly revealed others had already taken some. She guessed the catering budget matched the same low quality as the web product they sold.

On an adjacent wall was a ten-foot-long white board with the letters VRS written in blue ink in what might have been a child's handwriting. The letters were low on the board as if the scribe could not reach the top. Eerily white from non-use, Fiona made the determination that it had been installed recently, maybe just for this meeting.

The wall farthest from the group opened to reveal a door. Two men entered. The first man stood more than six feet tall with a shaved bald head and muscles bulging from his unbuttoned suit jacket sleeves. He had the distinct look of a body guard and was not wearing protective gear.

###

Right after him came an excessively lean guy with a beak nose. The scant tufts of hair over his ears and along the back of his head suggested he might as well shave his head, too. They approached the trio as the guide shuffled back through the door they had entered. She glanced back to be sure it had a handle.

When she turned back around, Lean was extending his hand to Ebony in greeting. "How have you been, Ebony?"

Holy crap! They've met. That's something she obviously failed to mention.

"Hello, Miss." He looked at Fran. "I'm Hector Sanchez, ADARK President and CEO. And you are?"

Fiona guessed his introduction was to impress Fran.

Fran shook Sanchez's hand, gave him her name but not her title, Fiona noted.

When Fran took a step backward, she left Fiona to face Lean Hector Sanchez, ADARK President and CEO.

"Hmm. I thought we were meeting with programmers and techies today." Fiona heard her own nervous sing-song voice as she extended her hand to Sanchez. He wore no hazmat gear, maybe because he'd entered the room through an entirely different place in the building. Her eyes darted about, seeking hand sanitizer.

"Very nice to meet you, Ms. Fiona." *Sanchez knew her name, but not Fran's?* "I hope you are not disappointed to be meeting me instead of Franz?"

"In fact, I am, especially since I came with technical questions."

Sanchez gave her a humorless smile.

"Please, everyone, be seated." Sanchez issued the directive. He and the other gentleman took the two ends of the table, making it obvious no one would be leaving until they said so.

"First question I have is, why the monkey suits?"

Ebony was concerned and took the lead on that one for the group.

"Not to worry, my pet. The employees in this facility spend a great deal of time in and around what we like to think of as potentially hazardous levels of exposure. A short visit in and out is of no danger at all to you ladies." Sanchez used a patronizing voice and stared directly at Fiona while responding to Ebony's question.

I am not your pet, asshole. Fiona hoped this creep couldn't read minds. "When you use the term 'exposure' are you talking about computer radiation or something more dangerous? I have seen a lot of computer rooms and technology geeks, but none ever in hazmat suits until today."

"My dear Fiona. May I call you Fiona, or do you prefer Ms. Vienna? Is it Vienna or have you gone back to Smith these days?" *WTF. He knows I am divorced, my maiden name, and what the hell else?*

Fran interrupted with "It really doesn't matter what our names or titles are, Mr. Sanchez. We're here to figure out why the hell you sold us a website that we cannot make even the slightest updates to on our own. We hired Fiona to be a web specialist, and she says she cannot even change the date or time on the thing. I asked for a calendar feature so that my press releases could be read online alongside our community calendar, and Fi says no way."

"Would you like for me to send a technical assistant to your office to help get you trained and…?"

"Cut the crap, Mr. Sanchez. I know how to code a web page, update calendars, FTP pages and overwrite code in an open source environment, but what you sold VRS is a freaking template."

Just as Fiona was getting started and opening her folder of questions, a buzzing sound came from

Sanchez's vicinity. He pulled out a flip phone, circa 1995, and gave it a wrist snap to open it.

"I am terribly sorry to cut our meeting short today, ladies, it seems there is an emergency elsewhere that demands my attention."

Without so much as another look, Sanchez stood abruptly, had the wall open up, and disappeared through it. The trio were left in astonishment, alone, meeting adjourned.

"Well, if that wasn't the most freakadelic set of characters I have ever laid eyes on," commented Fran without hesitation. "Get me the hell out of here."

"Thank god the door hasn't got us locked in," Ebony was already up and twisting at the doorknob. "Let's get."

"You knew him?" Fiona was accusatory, too stunned to have even stood up just yet.

Chapter 12

James stood in the doorway and watched Cruz Denning, Vice President of Technology for VRS, working furiously at his computer, and checked his watch. *I'll give you eight minutes,* he thought, grinning internally, wondering if the man would notice him at all.

Unlike the hundreds of new-hires, Cruz knew his business, which meant he had his work cut out for him. Denning had the tough task of keeping the systems up and running for a power grid that crisscrossed three states and nearly 600 miles of territory. James knew he resented the fact that the company continued to add incompetent employees to support running the administrative side of the business.

James looked at his watch. Bored with the wait, he rattled the keys that hung from his Liangery leather belt loop carabiner.

"Oh, hey, how long you been standing there?" he asked.

"Set the timer on my watch for eight minutes. You got about eighteen seconds left. I know how you computer geeks hate to be interrupted when you're in the zone."

"I'm the only one able to clean up the hornet's nest from our last shutdown." Cruz gave a huge exhale.

James chuckled. "I got places to be and butts to kick as well. What the heck is so gripping there, mate?"

"Freaking ten guys assigned to every shut-down, and here I am doing their work. Worse, I'm reconfiguring their fuck-ups." He sighed. "What can you do me for?"

"How'd you guess?" James replied. "I got something for ya. I think you're gonna like it, too."

"Oh, please. That black bean garbage you tried to pawn off on me last week had me crapping out purple an entire week. Not cool, man. Your wife made that shit?"

"Fuck you, don't talk about my wife like that. I made that chili and it was damn delicious. Your pansy ass probably needed a bit of a cleanse. All that drive-through slop you eat all day."

James knew that one perk of being the boss included any given number of underlings who would sit in the Taco Hell or Mickey Dee's line for you at noon time. Cruz took full advantage.

"Yeah, yeah, whadda ya need, old man?"

James understood Cruz's reason for the age-slam. The man was busy. VRS had enough 60-somethings with little or no tech capabilities assigned to attempt CAD and Internet issues to have an entire 40-hour work week of fixing screw ups. But he also had the added pressure of keeping the grid up and running, too.

"I got one for you this time. Serious shit." James pulled out one of the leather cushioned chairs from in front of Denning's large walnut desk. He ran his hands over the arm rests. "Nice digs you got here. My ass sits on a plastic roller from IKEA, or some shit out there at the plant."

"Don't get at me about this swanky set-up. You got an office up there on five you never set foot in. It probably has the same chairs, my friend."

"Yeah, air up there ain't right. People all breathing down each other's backs. Corporate ain't never been my comfort zone. Shoot, leather is cold as hell in the winter time, too. It makes no sense that the cloth seats in my truck cost me extra. Go figure."

"That freaking all-wheel-drive ritzy office on golden rims you're calling a truck?"

James smiled at the thought that the truck was more his office then any room inside a building. He doubted any indoor office would ever be comfortable enough for him. "Fine ride, too. It beats getting holed up with four walls all ding dong day."

"Okay, old timer. What is it you think you have for me? This report is due by end of day."

"Right. So, you remember how I told you about that chick making map books for all our line guys being good with computers, too?" James slid to the front of the large chair in excitement.

"Yeah." Cruz's skepticism showed. He tended to group all graphics people into one category: the user-friendly apps crowd. He had complained often enough that none of them ever understood file transfer protocol or systems functions.

"Well, she's officially ours now."

"Ours?"

"Reed put it to HR to create a position for her here at headquarters."

"Okay. How exactly does that do me any good, Mister 'I-got-something-for-you?' Sounds like another dead weight around here. Helena will likely be asking me to set her up with a CPU and big screen. I'll put Ted on it."

"No, no, no. You're not following me."

"In fact not, man, and I got work to do."

"Dude, listen."

"Did you seriously just call me dude?"

"She knows," James said.

The weighted pause and direct stare held Cruz's attention.

"O R?" Cruz's brows furrowed.

"Yes sir, O freaking R." The two shared a look of alarm "Got time for a taco now, compadre?"

"Gimme a sec. Shit. Seriously, James, you need to be straight with me right now because…"

James interrupted with: "Straight as a mother-fuckin' arrow, you hoser."

O R, or Operation Retirement, was the incognito name for Reed's master plan. The entire idea hinged on getting a transmission energy company, and sister maintenance operations, up and running, ready to sell back to either Midwest Energy Holdings or another private entity before the changing of the guard in DC.

The government contract for making nine cents on every dollar was only good as long as the current administration in Washington remained in power. Politicians in environmental, economic, and energy cabinet posts did not often survive under a new regime. The upcoming election year kept everyone on the inside on high alert for a potential cut and run. If the groups were exposed before going public, or if they sold to an unwitting foreign conglomerate at triple its initial value, everyone would lose the golden parachutes they were banking on.

Cruz tapped out a message to his assistant to finish proofreading the code and he'd be back in an hour.

She got the message and bounded through his doorway almost instantaneously. "You know I can't proof that shit, Denning."

"Good to see you too, Marina," James popped out from behind her. Marina jumped, shrieked, and then started laughing.

"Oh, for the love of stars, James. You scared the crap outta me! Now I get it, a taco craving. Just make it quick you two, I can feel Reed breathing down the air ducts on us today, it's freaking creepy. This report..."

"The report is nearly ready, Mar. Run it past Javier and then come in here and send it from my machine. I may not make it back in this afternoon." Cruz began loading a few papers into his go bag.

"Taco AND margaritas, huh? Have one for me, boss." She turned to James. "Catch you on the flip side, Captain J."

James smiled. He liked her "Captain J" much better than when Reed called him "Sir James." Hers held respect, not ridicule.

"And remember," she continued in her mother hen voice. "No drinking while driving the company vehicle, bruh. Call me if you need a lift. I'll send you a Lyft." She laughed at her own pun.

The two men exchanged glances and strode out right behind her. Neither one uttered a word until safely outside the building. Both knew better.

They were well aware of the cameras and bugs that had been planted throughout the entire building during construction phase, of course, under the guise of security measures. Cruz had even helped to install a secret walled-in control center off the bathroom from Reed's luxurious fifth floor office suite.

Once, after its construction, Cruz saw the inside of that room, a necessary move since he was vice president of technology. Reed showed him his creation with pride. Cruz came away filled with an entirely different emotion, once he realized he was poised to take the fall if Reed's game was exposed.

When Reed insisted that even the men's and women's bathrooms include holographic relay transmissions, the man gave him some bullshit about this being an at-will state for employees. Reed lobbied that everyone who signed his contract knew that their every move would be watched and recorded. He said he legalized the invasion of privacy in the fine print, giving them the dollar signs in much larger print. He made sure they'd receive much more than in any previous employment. Reed assured him that they would happily accept being chronicled to get those big paychecks. But both Cruz and James knew all of it was precarious and, no matter Reed's assurances, not legal at all.

As they headed for the parking lot, James recalled his last conversation with Cruz, voicing his frustration with Reed. He described his position as maintenance foreman at Midwest Energy, how it was never fun, but it never scared the daylights out of him like this situation. Billions in startup funding, millions flowing in from "planned blackouts" and crazy made-up maintenance work orders to "repair" an unbroken grid kept him under constant stress.

Cruz responded with his own concerns about the bogus website that Reed and his cronies paid nearly fifty grand for. A complete sham, no more than a basic template, in fact. Fixing that was certainly not fun. And, yes, it was scary too, being the one to clean up the huge puddles created by the whole scheming and skimming plots.

James, Cruz, and Ebony were all in from day one of VRS and ACME. The trio made up one quarter of the original twelve that became Reed's new venture. His insane growth by adding of hundreds of people was sure to be the recipe for disaster.

Even worse, all three had the leaked information circulating in the rumor mills. No one wanted to be on board this sinking ship, already aflame with faulty wiring, too many "accidents" and dead bodies—literally. Only one result satisfied them. Many of the simpleton add-ons had quit.

The freight train named Reed Jacob continued speeding out of control on the tracks, too late for braking or realigning the route. He and Cruz had vowed to keep each other informed when they thought it was time to jump ship. He hoped Ebony had made herself a way of escape, and that she had included Fiona with it. Fiona was a good kid, not responsible for the company's CEO's failures. Unfortunately for Ebony, James' plan only included Cruz.

All three of them were at risk. In one way or another, they were Reed's prisoners. James wanted his nice retirement. Cruz suffered a gambling addiction. Ebony needed to support her son.

James didn't envy her position. As Reed's one and only confidant, Ebony knew everything. She knew each contrived detail, from maintenance to computers. In addition, she knew about each one of his adulterous affairs. James was sure she hoped she had gathered enough dirt on Reed to protect herself, when push turned into shove.

Chapter 13

James sat at the back of the bar nursing a beer, a ball cap pulled low over his forehead. Patty's Irish Pub was the place to go to gauge the temperament of a particular segment of his workers. He paid special attention to Patrick, who was the self-appointed leader of this crew.

They sat at a poker table in the back room. James had inserted a poker chip in the hinge side of the door, preventing it from latching. From his table, just outside the door, he hoped to hear everything.

Most of them were ACME, some former cable installers.

"Listen, assholes, how many times I gotta tell ya's to keep your motha fuckin' mouths shut?" Patrick took it as his burden to keep his men out of trouble. "I heard your old ladies squawkin' about Joe and shit. Enough already. Keep your damn bitches in line or you'll be next."

During the pause that followed, James imagined Patrick making eye contact with each one of his men, for emphasis.

"Full house, jacks over nines, anybody beat that?" one man said. His voice came out a little thin, as if "The Look" had worked.

Five out of the seven guys at the table were former co-workers from Comstock Cable Company. A company made up of entirely bogus service and sales, where stolen lines and hacked systems allowed for three solid years of pulling money from innocent victims who believed they were getting a better deal than Comcast, Direct TV, and other cable television companies the area offered.

Patrick, along with a handful of others, went to jail for stealing cable boxes and equipment, splitting lines, tying into legitimate cable lines, and selling off the tapped systems.

The employees, former cable installers, low level guys, had no idea why their company went belly up. Each one happily took employment with ACME as gophers and drivers, thanks to Patrick O'Malley.

Patrick trusted the one who hired him, Reed Jacob, which was why James made a point of spending a couple of hours once a week at the pub, listening, especially after Reed bragged about Patrick. Reed told Patrick to gather about ten guys, smart enough to keep quiet, dumb enough to not ask questions, he'd make him a supervisor, complete with super profits.

It wasn't good that some of the guys' wives talked about Joe's death not being an accident. Patrick, James knew, would keep his guys in line. James heard an edge to Patrick's voice as he chastised them, as if the odd lot was causing him an ulcer.

His mind drifted back to Operation Retirement. He began to wonder if he'd be more likely to see the inside of a cell. Patrick was probably clever enough to avoid another incarceration. He knew what he did for Reed was shady, but because of his lack of knowledge about certain legal ramifications of his position, he might become the perfect patsy.

Chapter 14

Head linesman and lead supervisor, Fort Muller, one of the chosen few, understood the magnitude of accountability lacking in many crew members at ACME. Unlike Patrick, his sidekick who had zero previous experience, he had moved over from Midwest Energy having completed journeyman lineman training. He knew the importance of proper training and apprenticeship, the intrinsic dangers involved in this job, and the nuances of the power grid.

He hated the bullshit errands James ordered him and his linesmen to do because of VRS. Some shady deals, on top of the accident in March, made him anxious to get some answers. That night he decided to go right to the top brass, Reed Jacob.

Fort entered the pub with a full head of steam, convinced he'd put an end to the absurd chores on behalf of the entire team at ACME. He saw Reed perched in his usual seat at the end of the lengthy mahogany bar.

Fort pulled a tall stool over to where Reed sipped on a bourbon.

"That seat is taken." Reed never even looked up to see it who it was.

"Fuck you."

Reed swung around, looked directly into the eyes of Fort, and immediately recognized him as one of James' top transmission line foremen. "Do you have any idea?"

"I know who the fuck you are. And I know what the fuck you're up to. I know how you hold James hostage with this shit, and I've had just about enough of it."

"Listen, buster. You and your crew don't need the OT pay? We'll find someone else to do the…"

Fort interrupted him. "I will go to the authorities unless you call off the fake blackouts."

"Look, pal. Whatever it is you think you know, UN-know it. And if you had half a brain in that big, bald head of yours, you'd see that 'the authorities' are the exact folks who approved this company from day one. Now get the fuck outta my face and take that stool with you."

Fort moved the stool aside, but stood in its place.

Reed took a long swig from his high ball. He glared at Fort. "I told you to shove off, Bozo. You never, ever address me that way again. Got it? Wait. You might want to apologize straight away before I…"

"What? Before you what? Are you gonna kill me off, too? You bastard." Fort knocked the stool to the ground and balled his fists.

Two large men appeared out of nowhere and restrained each arm, dragging Fort toward the door.

With a nod to the burly men, unspoken instructions were relayed. Reed turned back to the bartender with a snap and point, signaling another pour.

Aaron, behind the bar serving drinks, watched it all unfold in the mirror, his back to the encounter. Mr. Jacob was a generous tipper. No way was he taking sides on this one.

"Fort Muller, is it?" Reed's slurred words reached no one but Aaron. "Well, Fort, you're about to get a name change. Ditch, I'll call you Ditch after that little display."

Aaron shuddered with fear. He'd overheard one too many of Reed Jacob's drunken tales the past couple of months. He might not want to take sides in a brawl, but he certainly intended to inform James of this incident, if only to protect Fort.

#

Ebony and Fran worked furiously on press releases about a new Green Corridor Initiative VRS had initiated. Reed was incredibly proud of his idea to plant trees and shrubs along power line trails to beautify and mask tall towers in neighborhoods, as if greenery and giving back environmentally was his brain child. He also intended to celebrate every bit of it. As Ebony planned events, Fran penned press releases and brochure text.

Fiona, on the other hand, noticed she was not included.

Fiona felt the distance growing between her and Ebony, which began the day Ebony had revealed her poisonous relationship with Ben. Maybe she regretted have said too much. Or maybe she couldn't leave Ben, making Fiona's presence a constant reminder.

Fiona was determined to mend that rift today. She'd heard about the new environmental department cropping up, and offered the team her graphic abilities. She had helped create flyers, print and electronic, whatever the head guy, Jed, needed.

But before Fiona could approach Ebony with a similar offer, Ebony took her aside. "Fran and I are grabbing drinks after work today with the new environmental guy, Jed something. Want to join us?"

"Yes, uh, sure. Let me just find a sitter." *Jed must be behind this olive branch.* Without mentioning it to anyone, Fiona had befriended the environmental guy and been working with him since his first day on the job. He was a good guy, seemingly unaware of the impact financially planted trees had on the VRS bottom line. He likely suggested to Ebony that they all work together.

"Bring the girls. They can meet my son. Flapjack's Saloon in Brighton has an outdoor play area for the kids so the adults can get hammered while, well, you know. I'll text you the address. "

Yippee, finally, a bit of a thaw in the icy exterior.

#

A giddy Fiona walked with Jed out to her car that afternoon. "You did this, didn't you?"

"Did what?" Jed Jennerson gave her a look of such pure innocence that Fiona burst out laughing. As she had gotten to know him, she found out that he was not only friendly and inclusive, but a tree-hugging MSU grad who got along with everyone. From the beginning he'd welcomed help from Fiona on small graphic projects.

"You told Ebony to invite me for drinks with you all. I know you did."

When his look didn't change, Fiona scolded herself. *Why, oh why, even bring that up? Shut up and just accept the offer, you ninny.*

"No idea what you mean, but yes, Flapjacks was my idea. Like, I don't have kids, but you and Ebony do, so it seemed like a good place to meet up. You gonna make it?"

"Of course I am. Wouldn't miss it. Just texting my mom to see if she'll keep the girls so I don't have to watch the clock."

"Bring the girls, I want to meet them." Jed was a genuinely nice guy.

"That's so nice of you, Jed. But driving to Ann Arbor to get them, then back to the bar would take too much time. You all would be gone by the time I got back."

Fiona knew her girls. It was far too risky to have them among this crowd after all the complaining she'd done at the dinner table the past few months. *Oh, the things they might say.*

"You're the boss. See you over there." Jed truly was a gem.

Don't get any ideas fishing in the company pond, Fi. She smiled as they parted for their vehicles.

Chapter 15

Sitting in his truck one early morning in late June, James received a text from Reed. "Brown the toast."

Melancholy set in as he thought about all that had transpired on his watch, the loss of Joe just a few months back still raw in his mind. How much longer would it take for him to get things situated and sever ties with VRS? *Damned lawyers take forever and give so little in the way of updates.* He couldn't take much more.

James didn't like the fact that Reed always expected him to do as directed, without so much as an ounce of thought to what was practical or ethical. This latest request—shut down the power to a small grid section of Southeast Ohio—just a brown out, grated on him. At least it was toast as opposed to a much more aggressive item on their covert menu.

The order came from Reed to James, but Fort would be trusted with the action. Damn! It bothered James to have to use a pawn in these dastardly deeds, especially his next best guy.

He sauntered in to the warehouse office through the pit of linesmen, motioning for Fort to follow.

"Fort, come on in here, son. I got a project for ya."

Fort trailed as instructed, but remained standing in James' doorway.

"Got some toast to brown." James was matter of fact with his tone, and did not make eye contact.

When he received the directive, Fort put his hands on his hips. "When're you gonna stand up to him, boss? This is bullshit."

James sighed. "I know. Please do it for now. I'm counting on you."

"Yeah." Fort gave James a crusty look. "Whatever you say, boss."

"Fort, listen." James unwrapped a Tootsie Roll. "I know I said last time was the last time, but everyone seems to have big plans for summer vacations, son. We'll need your expertise, and confidentiality, of course, on this one."

Fort's look of disappointment in his boss nearly crushed James.

"It's because of Joe, isn't it?" Fort said.

"What do you mean?"

"You're runnin' scared, boss. You stay aloof, except on the warehouse floor, out in front of everyone. I know what I heard Reed say. True, he was flying pretty high, but when he's upset, things happen. So I'm assigned to do this bit of dirty work, and another guy will be assigned to the next one. You won't be caught alone, right?" He didn't wait for an answer. "He's gotta be stopped. You know he does. Giving in to these brown and black outs just to increase the bottom line is bullshit, and you know it."

Fort marched away, his parting scowl burning deep into James' brain. The man was right. He stayed in the warehouse locations as much as possible these days, to keep an eye on things, is what he told everyone. He couldn't be sure that his office there was not bugged, and ordered Frank and the guys to give it a good "scrub down" every other week or so just to make sure. Even so, he spent as little time as possible in the room.

He never personally handled Reed's demands anymore. Reed could not be trusted. James wondered how he compartmentalized, and showed no sign of a guilty conscience. Something about the way he sent out one malicious text after another agitated James' sanity every time.

Hell, he thought, his mind on Fort. *I'm disgusted with myself, too.*

# # #

In the *Free Press*, and online, news updates the next day stated Midwest Energy had reported outages across the metro area from High Avenue to South Acres and from Low Street to Jones Farm Road. Early reports stated more than 14,000 end users were without power for nearly six hours. Authorities credited VRS and ACME companies for clearing up the matter within a few hours. Both were being applauded for their quick reaction time and comprehensive responsiveness.

Many speculated that someone, somewhere, likely hit a power line during a routine dig without knowing it. After an icy winter and blustery spring, news media outlets, and on-site reporters found plenty of footage and digital photos of VRS and ACME trucks on scene with handsome crews. The papers gave the story the front page, three columns wide, with a full-color shot of ACME crews and rigs on-site. A VRS Community Response Van also showed in the photograph.

The story covered the brown out as a potential disaster thwarted by the quick work of ACME and VRS. Images depicted heroic pole climbing, and handsome fellows in AMCE uniform, VRS patches on left shoulders, practically posing as if for calendars.

The linesmen heroes restored power quickly in outages. The media portrayed them as building a more stable system of the future. They mentioned a black out that had lasted nearly three days a few years back, where no one took responsibility. They claimed it had lasted so long because Midwest Energy was run so poorly. ACME vowed to do better, remain more vigilant, and protect the community from any such occurrence ever again.

It may have been a slow news cycle, or the dozen or so press releases Fran had penned, but media coverage was plentiful, and Reed glowed with pride. He strode off the elevator toward his office with great gusto.

"Let's have this one framed up, Jennifer." He dropped the *Free Press* full color story on his assistant's desk. "Get James and I booked for lunch at the club this afternoon, will you?" he added. "Time to zest things up a bit!"

"Yes, sir, right away." Jennifer was a stunning and solid asset to the lobby outside of Reed's executive office. A true multitasker able to listen and serve. Didn't hurt that she was easy on the eyes and not at all inquisitive nor prudish. In a pinch, she served him well, with discretion and no back talk.

With a wink in her direction, Reed added, "Hold my calls." He stretched out on the couch in his private office, kicked off his Cole Haan loafers, closed his eyes, and began massaging his temples. So much to do, so little time, so many grandiose ideas to update James on later today.

Chapter 16

Fiona took it all in stride. They shelved the web issue, since no one wanted to cry foul to management. Instead, they used work-arounds to upload the latest news hits. She clicked along with file transfers, uploading images, resizing fonts and headers to fit the template she'd been dealt.

"Big time news coverage, right?" Mac from the audiovisual department, excited about getting his photos and sound bites uploaded, stopped right in front of her desk.

"Oh, man. Mac, you scared the daylights out of me." She turned to face him.

"What the heck is so scary, if you don't mind my asking? Hell, I do all my own mixing and sound bites at my cubicle. No one around here even cares if I work a side job or two on that screen." Mac sounded almost accusatory, as if Fi were complicit in his latest venture. Although she sometimes helped him with his side projects, Fi was working on a VRS project at the moment.

"Too funny, Mac. You know I don't care, but I was so focused on a gif just there, you caught me off guard. Have a look." Fiona turned the monitor outward toward Mac. "That and my trusty HP over here is where you'll find the very juicy, illicit details of the high school hockey program I spent most of my time today fixing."

"Girl, please. I got zero time for this. You booked the meeting, not me." He was jovial, not condescending.

"Holy crap. So sorry. Completely forgot, Mac. We were going to stream some music behind the Green Corridors planting video today. Shit. Well, let's do it."

Mac pulled up a chair and pushed an HDMI cord toward Fiona. "Listen to this."

It took a minute to twist the CPU around far enough to attach the HDMI jack in the back, an odd icon appeared on her screen. She tried not to sound curious, but she needed to ask. "Is that?"

"Exactly what you think it is. A new logo and soundtrack for my latest venture. My DJ-ing days are over. I am counting the days 'til this mother drops." The tune was catchy, the beat and lyrics caught right away, a mix of Motown meets rap, sprinkled with a hint of jazz.

"Wow! Good stuff."

Fiona was tapping along to the sound when Ebony reared. "Okay you two, why no invite for yours truly?"

Before long the trio danced out of the cubicle, stepping through the hustle with a few extra dips to the groovy tune. Fran and Jed joined them, then a couple of other office personnel. They had a real party going, just as I-Greg walked past.

"So, the marketing department kicks back and parties when there's been an outage? Here I thought only the overtime crew got this excited over outages." Without further comment, Ivan continued to his office, wearing a wide grin.

As he passed Marci's empty desk, he looked back over his shoulder toward the group. His eyes met Fiona's. Her party mood vanished. She stopped and headed back around the corner to her space. No one spoke of the fact that Marci had never returned.

Chapter 17

It was a warm June day and Fiona was overjoyed to have been invited out to the Falbrook warehouse for a bit of work on some map books. The atmosphere there was wonderfully casual, and the location about twenty minutes closer to home, today was a good day.

She had lunched with a few old pals at Charley's Place, and had been back at a work station about ten minutes before she heard loud yelling.

The commotion came from the break room. Five hired hands hovered around the short-wave radio stationed above the fridge. It was the only spot in the aluminum warehouse that got much of a signal.

As James stepped in, the men backed away from the audio to let him have a listen. Their eyes immediately revealed trouble.

Fiona noticed that James was deeply shocked.

"I don't fucking believe it!" he roared. "There is no fucking way Fort slipped. He was as surefooted as I am."

Another accident? Fiona's heart rate quickened.

James grabbed a Pepsi can from the closest table and threw it against the wall so hard it looked like a brown fireworks display. As he stormed out of the break room, his shoulder brushed Fi's.

His look of anguish upset her more than his outburst. "Shoulda told you to find a safer place to work, girl. Benefits don't matter when you're dead. He's gonna pay."

What the heck? Was he talking to her? Surely not. She didn't have a dangerous job. How could techie stuff get her in trouble?

At that exact moment, the memory of Marci flew into her brain. *It's about as life-threatening as secretarial work.*

She watched as Veronica grabbed his arm.

"James, don't. There is nothing you can…"

He swatted her hand off his arm. "Fuck it. I'll dig him out myself if I have to." He ripped the exterior door open with force. "Fuck him!"

"Fuck who?" Fiona approached Veronica with great hesitation. She wasn't sure she wanted an answer.

"There's been an accident."

"I got that part. What're you afraid he'll do?"

Veronica stared out the door. "I am so scared." She began sobbing, wiping the flow of tears with her sleeve, no words came out at all.

Martha strode toward them.

"Look, Fi, we got a call about Fort falling into a hole for a concrete footing at that new station. I'll take care of V. You take a chaperone. Follow James. See if you can keep him from diving down that rabbit hole out there."

"Sure. I'll take my car. Frank, you with me?" Fiona had worked in the field for months with Frank when she'd been in a consultant role at the warehouse. She trusted him. That, and job sites were off-limits to civilians, but Fiona had sweet talked her way onto a few.

This time was going to be different. She needed an ACME man on hand if there was a bit of chaos brewing.

Frank swiftly took the keys from Fiona's hand. "I'm driving." He held the door open for her, turning back towards Vee and Martha. "We'll be back. With James. Don't you girls worry."

A moment later Henry flew out of the lot and rocketed her CRV at top speed west on I94. Dodging in and out of lanes, trying to catch James, they reached Highway 275 in what seemed like a blink.

"He never shouts." Fiona feared the worst.

"Years without a reportable incident. Now this on the heels o' Joe's death? Accident, my donkey." Frank's face revealed nothing but stone-cold anger. "Fort was getting too close, and I do not mean to the tower."

The two exchanged knowing looks. There'd been a powwow of sorts, at the bowling alley after last month's picnic. The journeymen all but assured that someone was sending a message to the field. To say nothing of the antics at HQ. Rumors abounded that

VRS was in talks to sell. Frank was one of very few linesmen Fiona trusted.

"Frank, you don't think?" she began.

"I don't think, Fi, I know. Fort stormed into headquarters last month like he was going to take Reed down personally. This damned tower is basically a phony with no real grounds for going up. As if any of us would dare second-guess all the freaking fake towers going up over the past eighteen months. Fort basically signed his own death warrant, the idiot. And don't think for a second that it's beneath Reed Jacob to hire out a killin,' 'cause I know of plenty. Around here you do what you're told, cash them paychecks and hush-bonuses. You play nice or get out."

"I was just talking to…"

"Stop. Not another word, Fi. You and I got nothing to gain by stating the obvious. Hell, if we were in a company truck, each and every syllable you uttered would be transcribed through to headquarters. Fools, all of these kids with a GED or better, thinking money grows on trees. Spend money to make money may as well be the company motto."

"Well, shoot, Frank. Can't we do anything?"

"We can and we will, darlin.' You gotta stay out of it, though. Fort slips into a concrete death trap not ten days after his little rant. Message is loud and clear, kid. Say nothing to no one. I mean nothing.

Serious as a heart attack, kid. You don't know the half of it."

"Have you told Laurel?" Fiona had set Frank up on a date with her pal a few months back. According to Laurel, things were pretty hot and heavy. "She texted me last week about you being stressed out about something you refused to talk about. Does she?"

"Listen, Laurel and I are doing our thing. Got nothing to do with my job here at ACME. Now that you are officially an emp-loy-ay at VRS, it'd behoove you to keep a low profile yourself. Authorities decide to ask you what you know about the number of towers in relation to the lack of increase in power to the grid, you know nothing. You hear me?"

"I already had my hand slapped on that note, loud and clear to me. Honestly, I was just trying to ride out my one year with VRS to tell my mother I was 'employable.' Then I planned to quit. Now that Ebony is in a fix with her ex, well, live-in boyfriend who won't move, I feel like I gotta see this through till... Well, crap. At least until the holidays, Frank."

"Good idea. Now then, left or right on the old barn road?"

"Crap, I took my eyes off the map back there."

"Never mind, kid. Lookie here. Firetrucks leaving the scene. Plenty of blue lights flashing ahead to the right. We've got us a genuine three ring circus."

Fiona saw no less than three media vans, dozens of spotlights, rescue vehicles, an ambulance. Off the side of the road, slumped over the steering wheel was James. Frank honked the horn of Fiona's Honda and watched James slowly lift his head toward them. His eyes were swollen red from tears of defeat.

Chapter 18

Riddled with guilt, James met Fiona's eyes, begging her to forgive him. He never should have suggested she work at VRS. Would she be another casualty like Fort? *I should have insisted that Fort take leave. Maybe I should have fired him.* That's what his men expected. You talk; you get fired. Simple. But he never expected to find his second right-hand man face down, drowned in a pool of concrete. *Reed is killing me by taking out my guys. Bastard.*

Money kills.

Fiona attended a service for the fallen linesman a week later. She was intrigued by the saying "chaidh uir air suil Odhrain." The words were printed on the memorial handout just below his full name, as well as scribed under his name on the poster-sized photograph of Fort next to an empty casket.

She Googled it when she returned home that night. Her body quaked involuntarily as she read a translation. According to a blogger, the legend of St. Oran, "Earth went over Oran's eye," referred to a man volunteering to be buried alive. Tears flowed from her eyes. Grief or fear? Uncertain as to what she felt, she let them pour.

Chapter 19

The five day annual Independence Day celebration always centered on a big family picnic hosted by VRS and ACME. An entire city block was reserved for them along the route of a Summer Cruising event where enthusiasts paraded their beloved automobiles, some old, some new, for an entire week. The fifties-style bash filled the streets with classic rides from all over for the festival.

On Wednesday, the first of July, Fiona decided to stop by the site after work and watch the set-up crew at work. Most of the guys would be from the warehouse, and she hoped to see some of them. She missed them, and she missed working there. *Less and more,* she thought. *I currently have less work, but miss the more actual projects and support. I also had work that gave me a sense of pride.* She frowned at that thought. *Remember the benefits, Fi, stay a year to qualify for Cobra, the only thing keeping me here.* She wanted the year to be done.

When she got to the site, she found the VRS / ACME team had nearly finished. The way the team had placed everything impressed her. VRS sponsored street rods and delighted everyone with rides down the boulevard. ACME rented a corner lot that hosted a chili cook-off style barbecue. There were rigs in place for families to enjoy bucket truck rides, but the moment she saw the bounce houses, she knew the girls would be delighted with this year's event.

Most of the staff saved their vacation days to either take the long weekend off or at least come to the party. Fiona chose to do both. She needed time with the girls. She also needed to give the girls a chance to meet Wright. He promised to join them there. She wondered what the girls would think of the four of them enjoying a bucket ride together, especially what they would think of Wright.

At the moment, the set-up crew was taking a break. They had fired up one barbecue grill, complete with a slew of burgers and dogs sizzling on it. They lounged behind a brick building adjacent to the party site. She didn't know most of these guys, so she decided to hang back behind one of the trucks before any of them noticed her. These were not Frank's men.

I need to get back to my car, she thought, just as a large, bullheaded Carhartt clad man, obviously loaded, began pushing and shoving his way toward two crewmen seated away from the group. He stormed right past Fiona, not seeing her. She was thankful for that. It was not her intention to eavesdrop, but she couldn't help but overhear.

"I heard what you said, asshole. And you too." He eyeballed a couple of men who were speaking amongst themselves on the back of a flatbed truck. "Come over and tell me to my face."

"You're full of shit, Jeff. We're talking about who gets with Ruby next."

"Bullshit. You think I pushed Fort."

"Have another beer, buddy," one of the guys said. "Bill here was telling me about that pole dancer you took home last week."

I definitely don't need to be here, she realized. But the reference to Fort's accident cemented her feet below her. She might just be looking at the one who pushed Fort into the tower footing.

Jeff knocked the two guys and their beers from the truck bed and threw a few wild punches. Two additional crewmen jumped in, trying to hold Jeff back, but more men piled on, until about fourteen were slugging it out.

It was almost no time before a shot rang out, followed by an ear piercing cry of agony. Fiona jerked back, making sure she was well hidden. She glanced at her car. She wondered if anyone would see her if she were to attempt to cross the picnic area.

"I was just tryin' to stop the fight," one man from the middle of the crowd whined. "I didn't mean to hurt no one."

Fiona peeked ever so slowly around to see a crowd had circled someone. She watched as they helped someone to his feet and amble away. They whispered among themselves, an eerie quiet after such a ruckus. The next moment they disappeared behind a brick building.

One of the warehouse foremen named Smith Wilson, she thought, looking just as drunk as the rest, approached the scene.

"All right, what's going on here?"

"Mac's been shot," she heard one of them say. "It was an accident, I think. I heard Bart say he was just trying to keep the noise down."

"Firing a gun keeps the noise down?" Smith scowled.

Only a drunk would think like that, Fiona thought.

"That's what he said."

"Damn shame." He bent over, maybe examining the man down. Fiona didn't dare look again. "Poor Mac."

"Yeah. Wrong place. Wrong time."

"Well, accidents happen, boys. Let's clean up this mess."

"But Mac…"

"Any injury, on or off the job site, affects everyone's chances for bonuses. You all know that. Can you imagine what a dead body from the home office would mean? He was only part-time. Stumbled in the line of fire, maybe."

"What d'ya mean?"

"I'll notify Patrick," Smith continued. He strode to one of the trucks and grabbed an ax. He threw it toward the bewildered crew. "You all clean this mess up. You know, the way they do in the movies. Barbecue the mother effer."

Fiona guessed everyone was just drunk enough to believe this made sense. Her heart sank as her stomach lurched. *Ohmygosh Fi, do not throw up!*

While the men busied themselves, she crept to her car. She moved slowly around the edge of the park as opposed to taking the more direct route where she'd surely catch an eye. Once she was safely in the car, and a block away, she pulled over and dialed Wright. She was careful to give him simply the basics so she could get out of there as quickly as possible.

Next she called James.

Chapter 20

James parked himself in his customary seat at Danny's Irish Pub, beer in hand, at the table behind the door, the poker chip firmly placed.

"Urban legend," one of the men inside the room said. "No one just barbecues a buddy."

"Yeah," agreed another.

James wondered who was in the room. As usual, he arrived late so as not to be noticed. Smith walked right past his table without seeing him he was so focused on talking to Patrick.

He entered the room, not quite shutting the door behind him.

"Hey boss, you got a minute?"

James expected Patrick to answer, but the next voice he heard was Reed's. *What the heck? Reed never steps   foot   in   this   dive.*

"If you need to talk to the boss, pal, you're looking at him." Reed loved it when the ACME boys didn't recognize him out of his suit and tie.

"Sir?"

"Go ahead, Smith." Patrick's voice. "Whatever you got to say, this here's a tight ship of sealed lips."

"You boys all ready for a big party weekend? Maybe we come on out of this air-conditioned icebox and join you for an early round of barbecue." Reed laughed.

"Sir, if I might have a word with you. Alone."

James wasn't sure which person Smith addressed.

"Oh, for crying out loud, buddy. Spit it out." Reed was not one to be left out of any loops.

"Look Smitty," Patrick said. "This here's Reed Jacob. You know, VRS head of clan. He's cool."

A long pause followed.

"Okay, my friend. Let's take this outside," Patrick said.

"Like hell you will." Reed's loud protest was almost a shout. "Spit it out, you retard. Anything you say to Patrick will be relayed directly to me anyway. Just because I'm not wearing Carhartt or Dickies, you think I get shut out? I own you, boy. I own all those peons you got out there getting the party started. Spit it out already."

Smith paused a bit longer before speaking. "Sir, there's been a shooting at the picnic site. Couple of guys bickering, one thing led to …"

"Shooting what?" Reed's voice was slurred. "Shooting what?" he repeated.

"We got one down and the rest of the crew is cleaning up."

What? James thought. *What's down? What's being cleaned up?*

"Nothing we could do but get to cleaning it up, sir. Mac is dead, Mac from your transportation crew."

"What the fuck?" Patrick sounded outraged.

"Wait a minute. Wait just one minute," Reed protested. "I didn't order no…" Reed stopped himself. "Shoot fire, we got a dead guy at the VRS picnic site?"

"I'll take care of it, Reed," Patrick said.

The three ACME men exited the back room. Patrick and Smith left the pub, but Reed stopped at the bar.

"Bartender, I'll have another." Reed muttered under his breath. "Who the fuck is up to what? And my week no less. I got four classics entered in the 'Cruising Over Fifty' category—refurbished at nearly a hundred grand a pop. Bastards had better not let this hit the streets. Ruin my annual. Idiots."

James slipped out behind Reed, leaving the bar unseen. He followed Patrick at a distance in his truck, lights off. He parked about a block away, keeping to the shadows as he stole toward the picnic grounds. It was full night by now.

He watched Patrick and Smith wander around the site, speaking to a man now and again. He crept close enough to hear their words.

"I heard it tastes kind of like pork," one of the men, weaving on his feet, said. "Tasty chili for the crowd." He waved toward the chili vats.

"The rest, especially the larger bones, we tossed into the bonfire. No body, no crime. No harm intended after all, just a minor disagreement over a hooker."

"Well done, men." Patrick beamed with pride. "Now then. You know the drill. Not a word, gentlemen. Not to your best girl, brother, uncle, cousin, or the family pets. Capiche?"

James threw up in the grass.

"We need a liquor run?" Patrick inquired.

"No sir. Plenty of Bud over there in the cooler."

Patrick stopped at the cooler and opened it. "Just beers, eh?"

"Just beers. All the barbecuing's been done."

James, still sick, returned to his truck and headed for home. *No body, no crime*, he told himself all the way there.

#

After Fiona's message, Wright called his supervisor.

"Stand down," the man said. "Not our jurisdiction. Not our problem."

"But a man may have been killed."

"That's the key phrase, isn't it? 'May have been?' We don't touch whatever goes on over there unless they ask for help, and you'd better take that seriously."

Chapter 21

On Friday, Reed ordered the entire VRS staff to attend the annual festivities as soon as they were able. Fiona, taking the option of a long weekend, returned to the office just long enough to finish up a flyer for her daughter's middle school fundraiser. She'd been working on it all week during her spare time and after people went home. She was especially pleased that most people had left for the picnic early. She finished the project with a list of donations and added a few more pictures before calling it done.

She glanced at the clock. Only three? She had time to pick up the girls and get there before five, if traffic cooperated. She'd told Wright to meet her at the picnic. She was on the fence about whether or not she wanted him to meet the girls. The picnic would be littered with "men mommy works with" so there would be no direct pressure on the meet and greet.

The girls were so excited to simply be going to a work party, especially when she told them about the bounce houses. She was home to grab them and back on the road without incident, but anxiety snuck up on her as she exited at the site.

"One bounce house even looks like a castle," she said, watching Ali's eyes sparkle. "So let's get a move on."

Late to the picnic of course meant parking in the rear of the back lot, hoping her car wouldn't be towed. The spot she wedged herself into wasn't technically a parking space at all. More anxiety.

The girls bounded out, hitting the ground at a run. It was a humid, hot summer day with gray skies that might open up to dump a deluge of rain at any moment. *Leave the umbrellas, you weeny. The girls don't care if they get wet.*

As she hurried from the back parking lot, head down, she noticed a group of guys gathered around a bonfire. *Odd day for a fire. It's gotta be 90 degrees and 90 percent humidity. Marshmallow roasting mid-day?*

She walked toward the carnival-like scene, thinking, *this entire area is body to body with moldering carcasses of men who believe the woman's place is in the kitchen.*

She laughed aloud at that thought. She knew what to do with those ass grabbing, gawking, pathetic excuses for men.

One woman was evidently riddled with low self-esteem. "Hey you, fat lard. Grab my buddies and me another round, would ya? Pronto!"

She gave him a delightful smile, then a middle finger and walked away, wearing a satisfied expression.

Wright met her at the table with her marketing peeps. Linemen considered her crowd to be geeks and corporate assholes. *Maybe we are,* she thought, grabbing Wright's hand in a co-worker hand shake to let him know this was the way the day would play out.

"Let me introduce you around," she said. "This is Ebony. She's the boss's main confidant. She knows everything around here."

"Truth," Ebony said with a grin. "You must be Wright. She talks about you, you know."

"No. I didn't." He acted surprised. "I hope it's all good."

"Not a chance," Fiona said. She turned him toward Fran. "Fran is our PR person, invaluable to the business."

"So you're the one who glosses over the lies?"

"Stop it, Wright!"

He laughed awkwardly as Fiona's eyes bore into him.

"Hot enough for ya?" Ebony grinned at him.

"Some like it hot." Fran winked at Wright, then tipped her head back and dumped an entire bottled water over herself.

"Anybody getting in the food line with me?" In this heat, she doubted she could swallow a morsel. But since the girls were already helping themselves, she decided to join them.

"Skyler," Ebony said. "Go with your Aunt Fi and grab us a plate, kid." Ebony eyed Fiona with a knowing look that said someone needed to stay put with Fran at this point. Why? She guessed she'd find out later. "I'll have a pulled pork sandwich. Add some coleslaw on it for me please, son."

"Shall we?" Wright took her hand as if he intended to escort her to a formal dinner.

She laughed. "We shall. Skyler, let's grab a Coke, then join the girls in the food line."

Fiona was grateful for the improved relationship with Ebony and her generous sharing of her son at a time like this. "Skyler, let's grab a Coke while we wait in that line."

Skyler looked back over his shoulder to be sure that his mother was okay with him having a soda.

"It's okay, son. Today is a party. We eat what we want. Grab me a Diet Coke while you're at it."

The trio strode along through lines of picnic tables, oddly quiet considering this party was traditionally a let loose engagement. Folks seated along the VRS section of tables were somber. The dark cloud hanging over the entire organization after Fort's death had some folks subdued, others completely sloshed. Reed, of course, insisted the party must go on, regardless. A fearless leader showed no reaction in times of hardship, steering the ship at all times with unwavering emotion.

Not one of these picnic goers had any clue about the Wednesday night misfortune. Except for

Fiona, James, and Wright. Still, they put on their game face and continued on.

#

Fiona and Wright tossed their empty paper plates into a receptacle near the fence line along Woodard Road. The girls had long since finished their meals and returned to their favorite bounce house, the castle.

"Hey, Fiona," she heard. "What the heck are you doing out here? Thought you said Birmingham gave you the heeby jeebies."

"Gabe Selleck!" She shook loose of Wright's hand lickety-split. The sight of Gabe always did that thing to her heart, where the flutter and flush rushed her body. "You need to meet an old friend of mine." She smiled, waved, and pulled Wright toward a break in the fence.

"Howdy." He gave Wright a long look. "What the hell?" He pulled Fiona off the ground into a giant bear hug. "You can have her back now," he said. "She and I go way back."

"Don't let me interfere." Wright took it in stride.

She liked that he wasn't the possessive kind, and leaned against Wright for a moment.

"My turn," Gabe said. "I want the two of you to meet my '64 Thunderbird girl."

"I knew you had a few collector cars, but I don't recall ever meeting one in person." She grinned at him.

"So," Wright said. "Tell me all about your Thunderbird."

Gabe needed no further encouragement. He dove into every single spec about his newest acquisition, including everything he'd needed to add and modify to make her run perfectly. Even though Wright was fascinated and asked many questions, Fiona tuned all of it out. Talk about cars bored her. She knew many girls who thought them as hot as their owners. But they did nothing for her.

She put on a happy face, smiled, and nodded at what seemed to be appropriate moments, but her mind drifted to James. She wondered how he was holding up. He had been like a father to her, keeping an eye on her while she worked at the warehouse, keeping the worst of the energy company thugs at bay.

"What do you think, Fi?"

"What? Sorry. My mind was a mile away."

"What do you think about the newest rumor of yet another VRS death?"

"What death?" She felt her face pale.

"Oh, come on. You told Wright. We were just talking about it, how frustrated he was that he can't get anyone to respond to what you saw and heard. Jurisdiction, my ass. They don't want to step on political toes."

She looked at her watch. "My. It's later than I thought. I ought to get the girls home."

"Won't work," Gabe said. "You need to hear this. I've been watching that bonfire. If I were to guess, a fire inspector would find teeth and bones in it once it dies down. They don't burn as well as the rest of a person's body."

"Gabe!"

"No, you listen. I know those guys. I provided some equipment to a company where they worked. It was a fake television cable company that made its money by piggy-backing on legitimate companies in the area, routing wires from established services to the homes they serviced. They made a killing by pirating from others.

"Did you know they offered me 'stock in the company' in exchange for hardware and a bit of software support? But I had a gut feeling about them.

"Turns out I was right. Dozens of low level investors were indicted when their actions came to light. I would have been one of them. Their scheme was so big it involved politicians and local law enforcement, which brings me back to that bonfire. Wright can't get police involved because they've been bought by VRS."

"How do you know?"

"I recognize some of the same ACME guys, convicted felons, the ones who went to prison over the fake cable company. They've been out of jail less than a year now, probably on probation. How could they work as legitimate linemen? It takes years of training to fully understand power transmissions and the like. They were never cable linemen to begin with, so they couldn't have been hired for their expertise."

"How did you get this job, anyway?" Wright asked.

Fiona sighed in defeat. "I knew Reed's daughter, Victoria. I provided her with wedding invitations and helped her prepare for her wedding next month. I had no clue that VRS was guilty of anything more than overspending. I... I never considered murder."

He patted her shoulder. "I know you didn't, Fi. Just watch your back." He turned to Wright. "Nice to see you again, buddy."

"What?"

Both Gabe and Wright laughed. "I've known him longer than I've known you, Hottie." His face turned serious. "Take good care of her. She's one of a kind."

Chapter 22

Ann Arbor, having plenty of local speakeasy type bars, provided Fiona with a number of places to meet Wright Danielson.

"Did you know about the cable pirating scheme?"

"Yes. And VRS is following the same pattern."

"What do you mean?"

"Plenty of startup cash. Rapid growth. Buying off politicians, and cops on the take. I'm thinking of bringing this before a federal prosecutor."

"He'll take it out of your hands."

"It's out of my hands now. I just need to gather more evidence besides 'he said, she said' to make a good case. But with physical evidence, such as human bones or teeth in the ashes of the bonfire, we'd have a reason to call in help, the local police and high-level officials be damned."

"What can I do?"

"You, my love, need to keep your head down. Back off and leave the investigating to me. Just keep reporting what you see and hear, and I'll find the evidence we need to break this wide open."

"Since I've been in the field for two years, I do have security clearance for the locations of all grid infrastructure. Will that help?"

"You do? Yes! Gather your maps and pinpoint the locations of everything that's live. In the meantime, I'm going to be putting in long hours off duty to research numerous companies, finding out where the electrical grid and power transmission mechanisms are supposed to be located. At a later date, we'll compare notes."

"And the money trail," she said. "Transactions leave records."

He grinned at her. "Gabe was right. You're one of a kind."

#

More determined than ever to solidify his exit strategy, James and Jeannie spent the morning discussing the details.

"What about Mac's death?" she asked. He left her out of nothing.

"I'm convinced it was as the crew suggested, a terrible accident. But by not reporting it, I'm complicit."

"You said they left no evidence."

"I hope not, but I did see someone poking around the remains of the fire."

"Doesn't matter," she said. "No one saw you, so you weren't there. What you've heard are rumors, should anyone ask."

He let out a breath. "True. Rumors abound."

"Better. Now, what do you have in place to protect your crews?"

"Not as much as I'd like. I'm staying until VRS goes public, after the first of the year."

"Yes, but what do you have in place?"

"Recommendation letters for those who need them, after the air has cleared. Some, believing the rumors, have already asked for theirs, especially the linemen who know what's going on. Many have already left, not wanting to go through the shit show in their future should they stay. I'm dealing with a skeleton crew of skilled workers."

"You'll manage just fine." She gave him a long kiss before shoving him toward the door. "Don't forget Martha's retirement party this afternoon."

"Oh, damn!" He glanced at the clock. "My, how time flies…" He nuzzled her neck. "Someday we'll have lots of mornings like this, where we sit back and just talk."

She smiled back. "I can hardly wait. Now, go."

Fiona, Ebony, Veronica, and Martha waited for James to arrive. It wasn't like James to be late for anything.

"His schedule is far more erratic than it used to be," Martha told them. "He's never in his office anymore. Works out of his truck, mostly. But this is unusual."

"Do you think he's in trouble?" Veronica asked.

Martha shrugged. "I don't spend any energy worrying about him. He either is, or he isn't, and there's nothing I can do for him with worry."

"Wisdom." Fiona laughed. "Just when a person gets a handle on life, they retire."

"Time to get out of here. Retirement is my way. What about you girls?"

"I'm getting married next year." Veronica grinned at everyone. "Besides, this fall I'm going to be working for my father's company. I really don't need the drama around this place."

"I'm staying until after the holidays, give my girls their best Christmas ever."

"I'm all set too," Ebony said, providing no details.

"How's it going with your cute Ann Arbor detective?"

"Just great. He's not only fun to be around, but he listens to everything I tell him, especially about our current issue here."

"Yeah." Ebony frowned at her. "You were a pain in the butt from day one. You knew there was a problem four months ago when you were hired on. I never thought I'd find a way to keep you quiet. Damn, girl!"

Fiona laughed. "Just give me something constructive to do, like tell a cop."

The women fell silent for a while, each caught in her own memories. Fiona thought about James, a bit of a father figure to her over the years. She knew he believed he protected his employees. She had liked that feeling of paternal safety. But now it was time to protect James.

When he had invited them to a lunch celebration for Martha's retirement, she'd jumped at the chance. But she hoped it would turn into a discussion of what they could do to stop Reed.

She knew James wanted her to keep her head down, but she wasn't that kind of person. She needed to be a part of the solution, not a cowering refugee in someone else's storm. "Just do your jobs, get along, have fun," had been his most recent advice. But she couldn't. Just last month Fort had died. Four months ago it had been Joe.

Fiona believed that an illegal quagmire explained the deaths of ACME personnel as well as Marci's accidental fall. To explore their legal options, the three plus Fran had created a weekend coffee klatch to share their suspicions, compile findings, and align goals for safe passage out of the halls of horror.

She patted the folder she carried. Yes. Today they would decide something.

But they argued about whether or not to include James. Because of his position as boss man, she believed they shouldn't risk letting him know about the information they had compiled. She wanted to test James out first, find out where he might lead the discussion, let him do the talking.

"Just got a text," Ebony said. "We're to meet him at the Cracker Barrel. See you there."

#

James found the women rocking in oversized chairs on the Cracker Barrel porch. He had to smile at the little girl in all of them, even Martha, who would be retiring soon. Today, he decided, he'd set the stage for keeping them safe, putting his foot down, if necessary. *Their lives depended on it*, he thought, as he remembered Fort. Being killed, just for speaking out, was unconscionable.

The Cracker Barrel hostess sat the group of five at a round table near the back of the restaurant. He delighted in their spontaneity, a lovely start to the meal. They complained about watching their girlish figures as they considered ordering the biscuits and gravy, and laughed at themselves. He was glad he'd scheduled this luncheon.

Just before they ordered, for some reason, Ebony excused herself to the restroom, unexpected tears forming in her eyes. What was that all about?

That was his first clue that their lightheartedness was an act. What was going on?

Fiona fidgeted. That was when he noticed she sat on a Pendaflex folder in her chair. After Ebony returned and the orders had been placed, an uncomfortable silence hung in the air.

To clear the air, James began his prepared speech. "Now, you ladies know I love Veronica and Martha like family because they've been with me forever. But I took a liking to you, Ebony and Fiona, right off, and that's saying something. My wife trusts me with the four of you beautiful women because she knows I see you as the batch of daughters we never had." He stopped and eyed Martha, a bit of a grin tugging at his lips. "Um, Martha, you're more of a sister."

Martha laughed and swatted his arm in make believe dismay.

"Jeannie wanted to be here with us today to salute your retirement."

"I wanted her to come, too," she replied, her tone soft.

"But this is also a double celebration, because we also congratulate Veronica on her new job, and on her upcoming wedding."

Tears began to roll down Veronica's face. She didn't look at all joyful for anything upcoming.

Fiona shimmied awkwardly in her seat.

Ebony cracked wide open. "James, I know that you know that I know."

His face must have registered complete shock, because Ebony reacted to it with force.

"Please don't look at me that way. It's not like Fiona and I just fell off the turnip truck. I've been here from the beginning, and she'd been out in the field with all y'all for two years before coming in to headquarters."

"But..." This wasn't the conversation he'd planned.

"Look, James, you did what you could to protect us all this time. Now we're pretty sure we got *your* back."

Ebony was like a hose running without any regulator. "We've been collecting, well... We noticed some things and wrote them down." She nodded toward Fiona. "Well, Fiona, why don't you let James see what we got?"

She frowned at Ebony. "I thought we were gonna hear him out first." But she pulled the Pendaflex folder from underneath her, opened it, and took out several sheets of paper. "No one needs to blow any whistles or anything like that. We just want you to know that we have compiled a shit ton of data, should you need it."

"Data of what?" James was genuinely stunned into a state of shock. No way could these three young ladies have any clue what Reed had over him.

"Transmission data logs, percent complete reports on projects in mysteriously non-existent locations, brown and blackout dates with weather conditions and statistical probability computations showing,"

"You have no idea…"

"It's all in here, James. We have backup copies of everything here that we may want to turn over to the FBI if things get ugly. This is not on you. We are taking care of ourselves."

Best laid plans, James thought as he listened to the group for the next three hours. They had all privately decided what to do with the parts of VRS that came under their control, researching information that made no sense, getting the broad picture and documenting everything.

Martha was the only one who remained silent. She looked as surprised as he felt.

As James left the foursome to get back to the warehouse, he let out a sigh of relief. These were a batch of incredibly smart women, certainly more able than the men in his posse to take care of themselves. Documentation, line drawings, memos, and collective thinking gave these ladies a fighting chance. He called Jeannie with the news.

Jeannie spoke before saying hello. Evidently she had been waiting for his call. "How'd it go? Were you able to find a way to protect the girls?"

"Not exactly."

"Not exactly? You spoke together for nearly three hours, James, and respond with 'not exactly'? You didn't send me as much as a text to let me know if everything's okay."

"We're all okay. Jeannie, I have to tell you, I'm flabbergasted. These women... They are so smart, so poised, so organized, so..." He explained to her what they had uncovered.

"I knew it. I told you so." Jeannie showed in her voice.

"Maybe so. You ladies, I have to hand it to you. You have a knack for coming together and rising up to your full potential when tragedy strikes. They're lending each other support in the face of the monster Reed has become."

"Maybe now you'll consider leaving sooner."

"Maybe, but this is so important to me, Jeannie. I want to see this through so that the good men and women of these two companies rise above this entire disaster. These women showed me that they are connected, strategizing, and willing to step up and actually change the lives of the little guy who freaking needs his or her job in this economy."

"Oh, James, that makes me so happy to hear." When her voice broke slightly, he realized she probably was shedding a tear or two.

James continued. "They gathered tangible evidence and expanded the rescue efforts for every one of the families that have lost... Well, you know who I'm talking about. They have a detective on their side. Although he's from Ann Arbor and working out of his jurisdiction, he's putting together a file that he can take to a federal prosecutor.

"Now get this. You know what a womanizer Cruz is, and how leery single women are of such a man, they still recognized Cruz for the genuine hero he is. When they approached him, he agreed to get electronic back-up files across the border into Windsor. He set up a designated secure server for them to access via the cloud. Even the simplest little oddity is now being recorded in real time. As they witness each small eye roll, each cash payout, odd comings and goings at headquarters, it's noted."

"There's more?"

"Yes, indeed! Turns out, they suspect Reed's most trusted ally, former FBI agent Larry Monroe. They say he has an entire underground crew working on some top secret project. They noticed him when they realized he was following them wherever they went, even when they went to lunch or on errands. What the hell could he think they were up to?"

"James, in the words of my favorite t-shirt you've always hated, 'I know that you know that I know.' It's so clear to me now. You were drawn to Fiona the day she walked into the warehouse as a graphic design contractor. Remember? You said, and I quote, 'That girl is a force.' Maybe, just maybe, she can provide enough force to be the tipping point."

"Tipping point. Your favorite of those damn Malcolm whatever books. God, I love you, Jeannie. We will survive this, I promise."

"Quit your dang promises and get us home safely."

James sent a text to Cruz Denning from his personal phone. "Time to make the donuts." It was their code for meeting up at the Tim Horton's just across the Detroit/Windsor border, away from prying eyes of anyone VRS or ACME related.

Right away his phone gave a ping in reply, a simple thumbs up emoji. James laughed. He thought back to the day Cruz convinced him to give this handheld smart phone computer-like unit a chance. He preferred the walkie-talkie like flip phone he'd had for more than ten years, but darn if Cruz wasn't eventually able to teach this old dog a new trick.

He tossed his cell back into the glove box as his laughter became tears. *We can do this.* He grabbed a napkin from the glove box to absorb the wet tears that slid down his cheeks. *Please, Lord, let this work.*

Chapter 23

James spent Monday through Thursday alone in the house he and Jeannie had built so many years ago in Browntown, just east of Metro airport. She now lived in their place in Florida, waiting for him to "settle things up." He missed her, but he understood. She was in a safe place, not about to leave, and she wanted him in that same place. With her.

Just a few more things to do, he promised her.

He figured he would stop at home to change his shirt before heading to the Canadian border to meet Cruz. As he turned into the quiet cul de sac, he noticed a long black Lincoln parked in the neighbor's drive. They were an elderly retired couple who spent the entire summer up north at their cottage on Gull Lake. The car belonged to someone else. The hair on the back of his neck rose up. He made a quick U-turn in retreat. As he suspected, the Lincoln followed him.

The radio sang to him. *"Bring back that lovin' feeling. Oh oh that lo-vin' feeling. Bring back that..."* He switched it off.

Time to make the donuts, all right.

He stomped down on the accelerator and ran a yellow traffic light out of the neighborhood. In his rearview mirror, James watched the Lincoln follow.

Hot damn. He looked quickly to see that he had plenty of gas, then punched the Hemi engine hard and fast.

About two blocks down, from the far left lane of the two lane boulevard, he made a hard right turn in front of a small sedan, narrowly zipping into the small shopping center parking lot. He heard hard braking and a loud double bang of vehicles hitting each other behind him.

He knew of an odd alleyway just after the Popeye's Fried Chicken where he could duck behind the shopping center. The rest of the buildings connected to each other in two adjacent rows of retail.

It'd be tight. If the Lincoln saw him turn in here, he would only have one way out.

He waited five minutes, ten, and fifteen. He slowly drove the rest of the way down the alley. The nose of his truck just barely poking past the alley exit, he waited another five. When he finally ventured out, no Lincoln followed him.

# # #

Safely across the Windsor border, James told Cruz of his close encounter. Reed obviously suspected James of going rogue in some way, and believed he could outsmart or outgun him. "I hate to think what that thug wanted to do to me," he admitted.

Cruz, ever the strategist, said, "Well, maybe we should set it up to bash things out with them. Reed won't be satisfied until he takes another go at you. If we arrange a showdown, that'll give him the chance. Us being ready for it, he'll take us more seriously. We just have to make sure he misses so it's obvious to the authorities that he tried twice."

"Jeez, man, now you're coming up with some really bad ideas. It sounds like you want me to be the carrot for Reed's target practice."

"Sort of. It's what I call a pre-emptive strike. Attack him before they attack us. And we *are* going to be attacked soon, since you're now being followed."

"We, meaning me," said James. "Reed has no reason to suspect you of any..."

"Yeah," said Cruz. "I didn't tell you yet, but Reed made it clear to his henchmen that he's determined to take revenge on you for getting away from him. I think he might use Larry to get at you, so he won't be blamed for it. No one in security is your friend, James."

"Shit, I told my wife we were safe from those guys because Larry was former FBI. I figured he was a squared-away guy."

"That's the way it should work, but Reed owns him, too. Plus, he has such a hard-on for you, he's willing to take his chances. He even asked me to look after you for him, wanted a camera installed in your truck."

"What?!"

"Look, James, you gotta trust me, who else have you got?" He laughed. "You should see your face, man. You'd think I'd agreed."

James shook his head. "I don't know what to believe anymore."

"I normally do what the man says, but I do have some self-respect. I choose to remain on the right side of the law, and let chips fall where they may. If, or when, Reed were to find out that I 'failed to execute' an order or two along the way, I'll quit."

"Quit gambling? That's his hold over you."

"I go to Gambler's Anonymous now. One day at a time, you know? Until then, you're still okay, more or less."

"I'm such a lucky guy. So, only half my head's on the platter?"

"Luck has nothing to do with it. Fate kept you out of the warehouse that day. Instinct and awareness on high alert ever since. Let's get back to the plan. The only way I can see to get them off your trail is to play like you're giving up. Either you let Reed think you're waving the white flag, or you fake your own damned death or something."

They spent nearly three hours going over what the ladies had presented, and planned a counter attack.

Chapter 24

Detective Wright Danielson looked over the documentation Fiona had given him. The boss couldn't throw all this away without looking complicit. It was time to make things happen.

The Ann Arbor Police Department was an anomaly. Peace officers and detectives fortunate enough to be assigned to the team in this relatively small town were highly educated, overqualified, and compassionate individuals. Almost all of them held unique interests outside of their daily police activities. Such was the case with Wright Danielson.

He'd attended the University of Michigan, acquiring a degree in education. When he'd been unable to find a teaching position that fit his salary and personal interest requirements, he entered the police academy. Having a judge for a father, and a scientifically officious mind, he spent much of his off-duty time reading and researching. Topics that intrigued him were space and time travel, electrical and nuclear power, and new scientific discoveries on the world stage. He even had a file folder in his home office on stem cell research.

He also enjoyed understanding how the government heavily funded some companies and not others. Long before he met Fiona, his quest for knowledge took him to VRS, a promising company to invest in. He'd clipped a few articles and slid them into a folder he labelled *Companies to Watch*.

Every so often he would invest a grand or two into one or more of these start-ups. Almost none of them showed returns like VRS did right out of the box.

It was on his radar, when the serendipitous call came in from an employee there. She was referred by a friend of a friend. The recording was still in his answering machine.

The female voice on the machine contained an undeniable fear component. The uneven tone, the slight whispering of the words, "Need to talk in private," stirred a bit of unease in him. She left no number to return the call, either because she forgot, or didn't want him to have it. He couldn't quite make heads or tails of what she might need from him, but decided he'd have a look at the company and its background just because.

He never did find the owner of that voice. But his research into VRS convinced him this was *not* the company for his investments. He found an unusual number of deaths and accidents in its wake that required further investigation.

Now he had the proof he needed to present to his supervisor.

Chapter 25

A couple of his inside guys summoned Reed to a secure field office near Detroit Metro Airport for a meeting. They were the men responsible for the takedown at the warehouse in March. *Shoulda been James, damn it.*

As he strode past Jennifer's desk, he paused. "Hmm. Say, Hun, could you please reschedule my afternoon appointment with Honeywell Construction?"

She checked the appointment book. "I'll call them right away. Later this afternoon?"

"Tomorrow would be better. After my lunch with my golfing buddies, I'm heading home." *Home. Every player in the world has used home when asked for an alibi.*

"Yes, sir."

For the past few months, it was looking like a clean kill. No one found evidence of the coil. VRS rented three buildings and two sheds to ACME out at Brownville. They used the sheds for storage, light production, and most of the offices, although James kept a warehouse office. As reported in the initial incident report from late March, only one building, number three, needed further inspection and an additional survey.

The inside of Building Three had been cordoned off for months, even after fire and safety inspectors scoured for evidence, searching for cause of death.

Reed's top-secret crew had successfully convinced authorities that they were simply using a Tesla coil-like safety device. An experiment, they told the investigators, to produce high-voltage, low-current, high frequency alternating current electricity. The acceleration of particles of metal shot out of the vacuum chamber via electrostatic repulsion and had accidentally centered on the metal warehouse door. The unfortunate occurrence during the night had caused one death and severe burns to another in the early morning hours of March 17.

He felt confident that the EPA would eventually rule the death accidental, once they filed their reports, if they ever did. In the meantime, Building Three remained closed, which irritated Reed.

He heard a rumor that investigators were "getting close to identifying a cause of death" in Joe's case. Evidently, the guy who survived, Henry, reported the shock felt much like "being struck by lightning." *How the hell would one know what a lighting strike feels like?*

Reed found the recording of Henry's testament and listened to it a couple of times before today's meeting. He needed to be ready for his conversation with the scientists who had developed the killer coil. Only Reed Jacob and these scientists knew about the new principle of physics he and the kill-crew had devised.

Reed prided himself on being cutting edge. Some Russian associates had turned him on to the technology years ago. The invention created force by accelerating pieces of metal material, propelled out of a central vacuum chamber via electrostatic repulsion. The weaponry of targeted electrocution was becoming reality.

Aside from some hokey *Star Wars* movies where force fields were created to deflect energy sources, there were no living physicists researching deadly force, for obvious reasons. Someday in the future, he planned to patent and sell the principles embodied in the technology.

Right now, however, he needed to keep his discovery hidden. Revealing it could lead to heady questions he needed to avoid.

These bozos had better not be late.

As he pulled around the back of the building, he noticed three vehicles parked along the gravel drive. He knew of only two attendees to this impromptu gathering. Jorge Niklaus, the lead engineer on the electrical science side, and Daniel Franz, chief steward and co-mastermind of the installation back in March. *Who the fuck invited an outsider?* Reed took a moment to contemplate simply driving off. It was important for the tribe to remain small. *Better find out what the hell is going on.*

Almost immediately, Reed felt his heart rate increase. Ann Arbor Police Department ID shown in the dash of the third vehicle. *Local freaking police just popping by? Way, way, way out of their jurisdiction here near Metro.*

Cops are retards and harmless, he reminded himself. Reed let out a deep breath and entered the building.

Once inside, he used a key card to enter through the foyer into the heart of the building. A few steps more and he again swiped the card to open a solid metal door. Inside were three men, all in plain clothes, puttering on individual handheld devices. Cell phones were not operational in this room, only digital content by way of VRS secured networks worked.

Who is this Ann Arbor guy, and how the hell is he using an electronic device in my secure lab?

There was a moment's pause before all three men stood in greeting. "Reedsy." Jorge used this nickname to annoy him.

"Good afternoon, Niki." *Take that, you geek.* Reed grinned at him.

"Sir." Dan Franz gave a more respectful nod.

Reed simply held up a hand in greeting.

Reed took three giant steps toward the unknown male, offering a firm handshake. "Reed Jacob, and you are?"

"Detective Wright Danielson, sir. I also dabble in scientific discoveries for fun on my off hours."

Science buff, huh? "Are you here with Dan or Niki?" Reed needed to know right off the bat which one of these two was screwing with him.

"Neither, sir. I greeted your pals at the door about twenty minutes ago."

"Twenty minutes, you say? So, this is how you make nice, invite yourself into a secure building, and access my network?" Reed felt his face burn with fury. "What the hell kind of investigation allows you to do this?"

"Sir, with all due respect, because it is ongoing, I'm not at liberty to say."

"Do you have a search warrant?"

"None needed, in this case, since I'm not searching for anything."

"Well then, what in Hades are you doing here? Jesus, Jorge, say something, for crying out loud. You called this meeting. What the hell?"

"Mr. Jacob," Detective Danielson said. "I wonder. Are you familiar with the 1977 document about Russian beam weapons? A charged debate regarding the technology, and its achievability, recently resurfaced." Danielson paused for effect.

"Quite recently, the FBI declassified documents on Nikola Tesla's 'death beam.' Tesla intended it, of course, for peaceful, protective purposes, never as a weapon." Danielson gave a chuckle. "I've been fascinated by 'death beams' since middle school, even doing a science project on laser beams and energizing them. I'm still fascinated by the subject."

"So you're fascinated with 'death rays,' a juvenile topic, if ever there was one. All teens are preoccupied with crazy science, superheroes, and villains with death rays." He laughed, but even to his own ears, it sounded strained. *Why weren't either of his guys interceding here?*

He continued his attempt at jovial bantering with the detective, getting nowhere for another five minutes. Nothing revealed the man's purpose. *Time to nip this little sucker in the bud*, he finally decided.

"Okay, Danielson, I think I get it. We're done here, and I would like for you to leave now." He paused but no one else moved with him, not even his own guys.

Danielson just stared back at him, a tiny smile curling the corners of his mouth.

Reed tried another tactic. "Still a budding scientist? You must have a price. What is shutting you up going to cost me?"

"Sir, I think you have me all wrong," Danielson said. "There is no price one could place on human life."

"What the hell are you talking about, 'human life'? You've been over and back about some electrical discovery. A budding scientist. Your childhood fantasy's, for crying out loud, about being the next X-Man or something."

Danielson interrupted Jacob. "Sir, does the name Joe Fitzgerald mean anything to you?"

Reed sank into one of the chairs at the table. *Mother Effer. He knows. He knows something, anyway.*

Danielson fought a grin. "I think you've given me everything I need for now. It has been a true pleasure, Mr. Jacob."

"Pleasure, my ass," Reed muttered as the detective left the building.

Fuming, Reed turned toward his two men. "Now, you will answer some questions. What was that man doing in this building?"

"We don't know, sir," Jorge said. "Like he said, he met us here when we returned from lunch."

"He was already here?"

"Yes, sir."

"What the hell was he doing? What did he say?"

"He showed us some kind of a paper that gave him permission to be here, and asked us a bunch of questions. We were careful what we said, boss."

Reed found no words to respond. *What the hell was going on?*

#

Detective Wright Danielson pocketed the remaining bugs he'd not had time to plant in the building. He'd hoped to be done before the two hirelings returned from lunch. Maybe he'd hid the bugs well enough they wouldn't be located. He hoped so.

Danielson chuckled. The cleaning bill he used to convince the two men he was on official business worked. *Security Clearance Cleaners, what a name for a dry-cleaning company.* He'd been using them for years, and had borrowed a ball cap from his buddy at the shop the day prior.

The cleaners specialized in working with law enforcement, priding themselves on the utmost secrecy. If a cop left something in a pocket, for example, it was returned in an opaque envelope, in the same pocket. They assured police that they never read any memos, or whatever they found. The item was removed, placed in the envelope, with the location of the item written on the outside of the envelope. A good company, in Danielson's opinion. And good cover for his dirty deed.

Chapter 26

As guests arrived for the wedding of Victoria Shae Jacob to Kyle John Spence, two flights of stairs decorated with tea lights, flowers, and small electrical transmission tower figures illuminated with the VRS logo, greeted them. No expense spared. The theme *Light Up Our Lives* blazoned into the heart and soul of the event, scribed onto napkins, matchbooks, favors. Even the photo booth had a small transmission tower worked into the geo-tag *Light Up ~ Kyle and Vic*. Attendees dined, danced, and celebrated late into the evening.

Fiona and Wright enjoyed a lavish four course dinner of steak and lobster, followed by a traditional seven tier white wedding cake. As the newlyweds cut the cake, the room lit with the flash of photos. A professional photographer hovered, shooting everything he deemed important from dozens of angles. She hoped to get some of those shots.

Reed spun Vic around the dance floor for the father-daughter dance. He glanced often at James and, for some reason Fiona couldn't fathom, at Wright, too. His security team, all wearing tuxes, guarded doors and spread along walls. Fiona accidentally caught herself taking photos of the guards, the room, Wright, and plenty of other "non-wedding" pictures.

Reed then took his wife Tulie for a spin on the dance floor, and Fiona ignored the rest and joined the festivities. *Lighten up Fiona, it's a wedding, a happy celebration, relax.*

Reed surprised James in the coat check room at about 10:30 p.m. "Where do you think you're going?"

"Just grabbing Jeannie's lipstick, pal." *Damn it all! The man has eyes in the back of his head.* "Great party."

"Say, why don't you drop that gloss to your wife, then meet me out back for a celebratory cigar? Pal."

James didn't like the tone Reed used. *Holy hell, how did "pal" spill outta my mouth?* "Um, yeah. Sure. Be right there." *Crapper. Jeannie's gonna be pissed, I promised her we just needed to show our faces, that I'd have her home by eleven.*

As James took his first steps out of the small room, his eyes darted left, right, and center. He felt his heart rate elevate. Even at a wedding celebration, Reed travelled with thugs for "protection" at all times. His body gave an uncomfortable shudder as he headed back into the main ballroom.

Nothing can happen at his daughter's wedding, James. Snap out of it.

If only it were that easy. James glanced over his shoulder like a grandfather clock every second since March, and it was starting to wear on him. As he approached Jeannie at the table, the look on her face gave him an indication that she saw a certain look on his.

"Sorry, sweetie. I couldn't find your lipstick." James offered Jeannie a wide-eyed look to accompany the statement. After thirty plus years of marriage, looks communicated more than words.

As quietly as she could muster, she said, "James, you promised."

"Yes, well. Turns out Reed has a celebratory cigar bar out back. I... Well..."

"James. You don't smoke." Jeannie fumed, her fury increased to a near visible heat. James had no reply.

With the next breath her face changed to one of defeat. She sank back against the cushioned dining chair.

James watched her fight tears. "Sorry," he whispered.

"Come right back to me, James."

###

There was a covered outdoor patio off the main ballroom, James expected to find Reed alone out there, as opposed to with a group.

He declined the actual lighting of his cigar by some unknown, flame-wielding suit, as Reed dove into diatribe about a VRS and ACME corporate restructure. Two bald men flanked Reed. Both were as round as they were tall, already two-thirds of the way into their respective cigars.

It no longer bothered James that Reed went back on his word to keep the entities entirely separate. His part in this farce would soon be over.

Reed introduced the men as the new Chief Financial Officer and Chief Operations Officer, in that instant replacing those who already held those titles. James wondered who they were, where they had come from, and what ruse Reed played on them.

Prior to joining the group on the patio, he had activated the record button on the phone Cruz had schooled him on a week prior. Making mental note of their posture, he felt no threat from these cheese puffs. Fiona's detective might just be able to shed some light on these two: Andrew Messing, the new CFO, and Jedidiah Mangham, COO. *Hope the recorder got those names, Jedi-what?*

James also tried to made mental notes of the tidbits of information Reed spoke about them, god forbid he not have the recorder set properly. He wondered if the thing could catch all this from an inside pocket of his jacket. Both men came from a recent downsize at some west coast operation. Both held impressive expertise in natural gas and energy trading or something of that nature.

Reed droned on. James' mind wandered to the hundreds of thousands of dollars each Reed promised them. Bonuses guaranteed as well. *Another couple hundred grand of income generated, check.*

Midnight arrived before James returned to escort Jeannie out of the building.

"Don't ask," he muttered, thrusting his chin at the two.

"Handsome devils," Jeannie offered with a sly smile.

"Devils describes them about right." They left the ballroom hand in hand.

Jeannie was in Ohio with him for the weekend. He didn't want to waste even one more ounce of energy worrying. He rolled down his truck window to keep himself awake for the long drive home. Jeannie slept peacefully on the bench seat of his truck. "We'll get there, my princess," he whispered.

Chapter 27

Two weeks after the wedding, to be away from the dark vibes at VRS as much as possible, Ebony and Fiona often lunched off-site. They changed up their routine, no longer dining in the cafeteria, breakfast nor lunch. Friday, with nothing looming or productive to do, neither planned to return until Monday after lunch at Shooters.

They spied the photo booth at the same time. Fiona winked; Ebony grinned and, as one, they headed inside. They took a few pictures in funky hats and festive props, laughter ringing all around them.

On the fourth and final take, their eyes met in a way that made Fi uncomfortable. "What is it?"

"Girl, if you only knew." Ebony had a way of holding it over Fiona that she'd never really be on the inside track at VRS.

"Maybe it is better that I don't know. You know?" But she hoped Ebony would disagree. She was in so deep at this point, what she didn't know could, in fact, hurt her.

A flash caught the actual concerned look between the two of them, catching both off-guard. When they exited the booth, they stood in silence outside waiting for their photo strip to drop. Fiona excused herself to the restroom, and returned to their table a few minutes later.

As she looked down at the photo on the table between them, Fiona decided she had waited long enough for any kind of a response from the woman.

"See you Monday?" She was doing her best to let Ebony come to her of late, as opposed to pushing for details as she had done in those early months.

The two women rose from the table, pulled on jackets, and grabbed their respective bags without words.

Ebony broke the silence in the parking lot. "Night, Fi. Get home safe."

Fiona felt uneasy as she glanced back over her shoulder at Ebony. "Are you okay?"

"Yeah. Yes. How about you drop me at my place? You mind?"

"Not at all. You leaving your car here all weekend?"

"I'll take a taxi into work on Monday." Ebony sounded like a younger version of herself with a pleading voice. "It's out of your way. If you can't, that's cool. I just…"

"Let's roll." Keeping it light and airy, she wondered if Ebony might like to pop into Starbucks for a coffee. *Maybe she's ready to talk.*

"Hope you don't mind if we stop at SB, I need a boost. Can I buy you a pumpkin spice latte? Pretty sure they are out already."

Ebony nodded in agreement. She was keeping something in and Fiona could feel it.

"Drive-through or going in? We have time before bus pick up, el oh el. So bold of us to not go back this afternoon, but frankly I've had zip, zero, nothing going all week."

"In."

Fiona parked the CRV closest to the front door of Starbucks, got out, and waited a beat for Ebony to exit and shut the passenger side door. *Is she tearing up?* Bleep, she locked the car.

She held the door for Ebony, and watched as she robotically entered the café, scanning the room with an odd curiosity. When she seemed to be satisfied she didn't recognize anyone, she turned to Fiona with, "can you spot me a coffee? I am cash poor this week."

"No sweat. It's practically not even money when you use the app! Grande pumpkin spice latte coming up. Grab that window seat and I'll place the orders."

A few minutes later, lattes on the table between them, Ebony let the bomb drop.

"They're bringing in new management," she blurted.

"What does that mean?"

"I don't know. I only know that Reed's surrounding himself with all new people. Where does that leave the rest of us? I have no idea. But sometimes I feel like a chicken headed for the butcher's block."

Fiona pondered the outcome of a Christmas for Alison and Lauren if she got sacked. It wouldn't be as lean as Christmas' past. When she started at VRS she opened a savings account for the first time in ages. *No bonus, no holiday getaway.*

"Y'know, there's only two of us left."

"Yeah. Veronica left two days ago. Now she assists her father instead of James. Martha has retired. Although Victoria wasn't really a part of our group, she was a good friend. Now she's got her own life, being married to Kyle. My, how quickly those two hit it off after I introduced them."

"Yeah. I should have had you around before I met Ben. I might have made better choices."

"So, what's your plan? I mean, if you leave?"

"I'm going back to finish my teaching certification. All I lack is the practice teaching. I can get that done this spring semester. Then I'll put in applications this coming summer for the fall semester. I really need to get a job outside of the corporate world."

"Good for you!"

"What're you gonna do?"

"Go back to consulting. It paid the bills before, just barely. But 'just barely' is beginning to sound very good right now." She took a sip of her latte. "We know too much."

"Truth. Way too much. Maybe that's the reason for the new management."

"Maybe."

They sipped in silence for a while. "Could you pick me up tomorrow for our weekly coffee klatch? I hate to ask, but I really don't like to be alone lately. I left my car at Shooters 'because I don't trust myself on the road lately. My mind is all over the place."

"I totally get that."

"Do you mind if I bring Skyler?"

Fiona laughed. "Not if you don't mind if I bring Ali and Lauren. We'll make a day of it."

"So, are you sure that's the only reason you left your car in the parking lot?"

"Damn girl, you're like a psychic or something. Nothing gets by you." They both let out awkward chuckles. "I saw someone poking around under it." Tears cluttered her eyelashes. "I'm scared, Fiona. Do you suppose your detective friend could take a look at it, make sure it's all right?"

Without hesitation, Fiona pulled her phone out of her pocket and texted Wright.

"New pact," she said. "Just between the two of us. We'll meet on Saturdays, like before, and watch each other's backs. Deal?"

"Deal." Ebony used a napkin to swipe away a tear that thought it could get away. "Deal," she repeated, this time with more confidence.

Chapter 28

That weekend Wright found a bug, not a bomb, much to Ebony's relief. He placed the bug into a small paper bag and made a note on it before placing it in his glove compartment.

"You're safe to drive it now, Ebony." He removed the plastic gloves he had worn while searching for the thing.

"What're you gonna do with it?"

"Have it examined for fingerprints."

"Evidence?"

"It may be. But you have an ex-boyfriend who might feel malicious, right? We need to separate his possible actions with other possibilities."

"Oh. At least I have my car back."

"That you do. Are you all right?"

"Now I am. Thanks."

"No problem. All part of the job." He gave Fiona a broad smile. "Tomorrow night still on?"

"Still on," she agreed.

They returned to work that Monday, both ready to face another day.

To her surprise, Fiona found a note on her desk from Ivan. She texted Ebony.

"Same," Ebony texted back. "2:00?"

"Same."

"I guess I'll see you there, then."

"Yep."

At 2:00, they found Fran already waiting in one of the chairs facing Marci's old desk. Ivan had never replaced her. It felt empty without the right person at the desk.

"You too?" Fran rose to meet them.

Before either of them could answer, Ivan appeared in his doorway. He was flanked by two elderly women in polyester, shoulder pads, and ruffles, the kind not seen since the 80s.

"Ladies, have a seat, please." Ivan waved the three of them to the opposite side of the table from him and his sidekicks. Fiona, ever the disturber, pulled out an end seat at the head of the table. Ivan noticed, giving her a condescending nod. "As you wish."

"You must be Fiona," the elder of the two held out a hand to Fiona while remaining standing. "I am Georgia Andreal, Senior Vice President of Marketing under Ivan." She kept a firm grip on Fiona's hand for an uncomfortably long spell, then added, "This is Florence Attaway, my assistant. She goes by Flo."

It took all she had to keep her mouth shut, thinking *go with the flow*. "Nice to meet you, Georgia."

"You may address me as Ms. Andreal, if you don't mind."

Flo and real. Go and Flo. Fiona smiled widely but held the audible laugh. "Curtsey or bow?" she accidentally muttered. *Oh, man.*

"Pardon me?" quipped Ms. Andreal, sending a dark side eye glare toward Fiona.

"Sorry. Nothing. Very nice to meet you both." Fiona avoided eye contact with Fran or Ebony for fear they'd all dissolve into uncontrollable laughter.

Fran stood up to extend her hand across the table. "Fran Marner. Press Relations. No relation to the football Fran."

"Football?" Flo looked confused. "I don't know what you mean."

Ebony remained seated, looking directly at Ivan. "So incredibly nice to have new senior marketing management on board." She then turned her eyes to the two newbies who had remained standing for some unknown reason. "By process of elimination, you likely know I'm Ebony Anderson. I am one of the original twelve founding members of Various Reliable Services, initially serving Sir Jacob directly. I am now marketing manager and responsible for all event planning activities. Why don't you ladies, and Ivan, have a seat and give us an update on what exactly a Senior Vice President of Marketing and her assistant might be bringing to the table?"

An awkward hour later, Fran, Ebony, and Fiona were excused from the room. Ivan, Georgia, and Flo stayed behind. As they left the room, Fiona heard Ivan give an audible sigh, followed by "I think I mentioned to you ladies that this wasn't going to be an easy transition for that bunch."

Because we know what we're doing, unlike most new hires at this place, Fiona said from within the confines of her mind. *How I want to say that aloud!*

Fran and Ebony, both furious, strode away too quickly to have overheard it. Fi decided not to mention it, to prevent the eruption of fireworks.

Transition, my behind, she thought instead. *More like a takeover.*

Ms. Andreal's few statements directly affected Fiona. Specifically that all web-based communications were on hold until further notice. The Twitter and web chat functions of the website had already been "taken care of" by an outside advertising agency newly contracted by her and Flo on behalf of VRS.

Just before she left, Fran, unable to keep the stunned expression off her face, said aloud, "Thankfully, at least my resume is up to date. Other companies, I'm sure, will appreciate a more forward-thinking employee."

Before she left, Ebony, her eyes boring into Ivan, told him, "I'm gonna talk to Reed about this bullshit."

Fiona took a seat in her cubicle and noticed a missed call from her oldest daughter. She took a deep breath and dialed home.

"Hello?" Allison answered the phone.

"Hi, sweetie, what's up?" Fiona asked.

"The pizza kits arrived at school today. Can I make some?" Allison was talking into the phone, but she could hear Lauren in the background saying, "Breadsticks, too. Tell her we want to make breadsticks, too."

"Golly, you know my rule about having the oven on when I am not home, Al." She paused a minute and made the executive decision to leave early. Today became a waste before it started.

"But, Mom, you said that Lauren and I needed to start taking more responsibility."

"Tell you what, set the oven temp to 400 degrees and put some foil onto a cookie sheet. I'll head home right now so that by the time I get there, we can put it in together. Deal?"

"But it's only three. You don't get here 'til six most of the time. Did you get fired, Mom?"

"Ha ha, pretty funny, you." *I hadn't thought of that. By taking the rest of the day off... Holy crap.* "I'm bringing some work home," she lied.

"Okay. But you always say you're on your way and then it's like an hour before you actually get here."

Allison sounded frustrated. Fiona could hear Lauren through the phone, adding "More like hours. Plural."

"I promise. I'm walking out the door. Right. Now." As Fiona said the last two words, her two brand new superiors turned the corner and stood in front of her desk.

Think fast, she told herself. "Jed," she said into the phone. "It will be fine. I'll be at the warehouse in no time. I'll recreate the files as soon as I get there."

"Who is Jed?" Allison asked just as Fiona hung up.

She shrugged at the two elders and began to pack up her laptop for departure. Neither woman said anything directly to Fiona, but as they got about ten feet past her, she was pretty sure she heard the words "time clock."

She scrawled a quick note for Ebony and slid it into Eb's top desk drawer. "Let's call them Go and Flo. Call me tonight."

As she passed by Fran's cubicle, she intended to make the same suggestion to her, but her desk was already cleared. She had obviously left for the day as well.

# # #

When Fiona arrived home, the girls had already put the pizza and breadsticks in the oven, set the timer, and were in the kitchen watching with the oven light on, quite pleased with themselves to have "made dinner."

"Early dinner! I love it, ladies! You two are growing up so fast." Tears filled Fiona's eyes. Allison was glued to watching the pizza, but Lauren turned to her mother with open arms.

"Are you okay, Mom?" Lauren was already as tall as Fiona at just 13 years old.

"Fine. I'm fine, honey." But the tears poured down like a flash flood.

"Whoa, what happened?" Allison turned to see the crying mother-daughter combo. Fiona broke free and went to the first floor bathroom, grabbing toilet paper to use as Kleenex.

"It's fine. I'm fine. It's just..." Fiona really hated to burden her girls with any of the nonsense of job stress or the VRS baloney. It had been about six months. All three of them in their own minds knew they had avoided talking about how the new job was taking its toll on Mom. Everyone hurts when Mom hurts.

"We hate your job, too, Mom," Lauren offered in a frank tone. "Just quit."

"Yeah, it's not worth it. We don't care about money. Stay home, work like you used to with all those randos stopping by. Call Gabe. He'll help. And he is 'easy on the eyes' like you said."

That comment made Fiona laugh. "But you always complained about the 'randos' and creepy people here at odd hours to work on websites, logos, whatever."

Allison interrupted with an impatient sigh. "Sure, there were some creepy people in our house, but at least *you* were here."

They dined on pizza and breadsticks, double dipped into the ranch dressing, and giggled about a few of the most memorable random characters from Fiona's consulting days. There'd been a chiropractor who always invited himself to stay for dinner. The coffee shop Fiona had traded a lifetime of free lattes with for creating their logo.

She had somehow stayed afloat, trading logo and web work with their dentist, her doctor, and even a few local restaurants. Many were trade. Teeth cleaning, gift certificates, you name it. Traded for ad layouts or design work. It was hard to argue with the fact that being home with them was priceless.

"Listen, I just have stick it out through the holidays, okay?" Fiona was trying to convince herself more than the girls. "Grammy loves the fact that we have benefits. At Christmas I'll get a bonus with some paid time off. If I can make it to one year, I don't have to pay back the signing bonus. Remember our trip to Rome and Venice last summer? That was all thanks to the lump sum check I got when I signed on with VRS."

"Oh my God, Mom. Listen to yourself. Money, money, money. How many times have you told us to never do anything because of the money?"

Ali was right. "You've got me there." Fiona took a moment to decide how much to say or not say. "Brush your teeth and get in your jammies. We'll watch a Harry Potter movie and pretend it's the weekend."

"Mom. It's 4:30 in the afternoon." Lauren gave her a suspicious glare.

"Yes. I'll pull the shades and make popcorn. We'll pretend its nighttime, and watch two in a row if you hurry up!"

"Soda with the popcorn?" Allison jumped up, heading for the fridge.

"Caffeine free. Root beer or 7-Up, you pick." Fiona was thankful to change the subject.

"Root beer floats!" Lauren squealed.

"Yes! Let's go before she changes her mind." Allison tugged at Lauren and the two trotted up the stairs with excitement.

Fiona wiped a few tears away before retreating to the pantry for the Orville Redenbacher. Root beer floats sounded pretty darned good all of a sudden. She'd add a splash of Kahlua to hers. *Six more months. Can I do it? Gotta love a good movie to take your mind away from life for a bit.*

Chapter 29

Ebony took deep breaths as she floated two floors up to the executive offices of VRS to speak directly with Reed. As she exited the elevator, an odd quiet filled the foyer in front of Jennifer's desk. No one in sight, she took a few steps toward the large oak desk. The door to Reed's office was closed, and she wondered if she heard something coming from the other side of the wall.

Her anger transformed into disgust. *What the hell is going on these days?* She turned around to call the elevator back and screamed as the door slid open. Cruz Denning had hollered "Boo!"

"Cheese Danish!" Ebony yelled, swatting at Cruz. "You nearly gave me a heart attack."

"Cheese Danish? Really. That's all you got?" Cruz doubled over in laughter. "I honestly thought I'd be getting Jennifer as the door opened. Where is she?"

Ebony didn't answer with words, just rolled her eyes and pointed at the closed door to Reed's office.

Wide eyed, Cruz mouthed "no way" as if he were a mime. He followed that up with the "finger into hole" gesture and a questioning look. Ebony shrugged and stepped past him onto the elevator.

"You coming?" Ebony held her hand across the elevator door to wait for Cruz to step in. She pushed G as opposed to three for the third floor where her office was located.

"You headed out or headed to the cafeteria, Eb?" The ground floor of the building hosted mainly the front lobby area, cafeteria, back exit to the parking garage, and warehouse space for odds and ends.

"Hell. I honestly don't know. My mind is racing in a million directions right now, Cruz. So much has changed in so little time."

"I hear you." Cruz could relate, literally. He'd been tasked with adding computer work stations for new employees nearly every week for over a year now. "Those two dinosaurs you just got? They *really* do take the cake. The oldest one said she wouldn't be needing the Microsoft Office Suite. She *actually* said the words, 'give mine to my assistant,' as if she had no idea. It was almost like when I said 'hardware and software,' she was thinking of concrete blocks and pillows. I feel for you, I really do."

"Reed is officially off the rails." Ebony stopped herself. Even the elevators were tapped with audio and visual. "You know what I mean. Growing too fast, sort of." There was a frightened look in her eyes, pleading with Cruz to assure her that she'd covered herself.

Cruz returned a look of complete understanding. Then he hid his hands from the corner camera and made walking fingers. He pulled her into a friendly hug and whispered in her ear quick, "I'll get off at one and meet you outside."

There was a half mile loop walking path and benches out back. It was chilly, but not raining. They could get away without coats if they walked fast. Once outside the building, and far enough into the thicket, they'd be able to talk freely.

Cruz could see Ebony entering the woods and kept a slow pace until he knew he was out of sight from the building windows. He caught up to her about fifty yards in, and they walked side by side in silence for a moment.

At the second turn into the woods, Ebony let a few tears roll. "I'm a single parent, Cruz. I need this job. I literally *just* got my loser boyfriend, Ben, moved out of my place. I just can't."

Cruz put one arm around her shoulders. The gesture released the waterworks and Ebony was now bawling into his sweater.

"What the fuck is going on in there these days?" she continued. "Are you seeing what I am? With all the new people, new vehicles, tree planting, money wasting?"

"Look, Eb. We knew what we were signing up for. In a way. Five years. Five years is what we all agreed to as do-able. You and I, we're just months away from being fully vested. We get out before…"

"Before what? Before he kills us, too?" Ebony was frayed. She and James, along with Fiona, Cruz, and that dreamy Ann Arbor detective were close to putting a case together. All five of them agreed that Reed was shutting down any people who were a threat to the exposure of his government scam. They all understood that he'd meant to kill James on the morning of March 17 when Joe inadvertently took the zap.

"Okay, okay, watch your use of words there, Eb. No one wants to kill anyone."

"Don't be daft, Cruz. Joe, then Fort. These aren't job site mishaps, for cripes sake. James knows he's next. Or was first. On some list it feels like. It's only a matter of time before someone realizes that you and I have been talking to outsiders."

Cruz had, in fact, enlisted a few investigators from across the border. He had a full-scale model and outline of what he knew, and how he had been coerced into cooperating with Reed from day one. *That damned gambling addiction, and all that cash.*

"I'm nearly a year clean from any tables, Ebony. I'm clearly in the line of fire, maybe even more so than James. I totally get what you're saying. Thing is, Reed loves you more than his own children, Eb. You got nothing to worry about."

"Nothing? You figure answering to a couple of power hungry old bags on the daily is nothing? That old one wants to be called 'Mizz Andreal,' for crying out loud. I'm too damn old to be told how to address some dumb broad."

"You felt the same way when Fiona started," Cruz reminded her. "Now you're thick as thieves."

"No. You're wrong there. I had a great deal of distaste for her, but she didn't come at me like that. Never like she was gonna tell me what to do, or run my days and shit. These two are so full of themselves. They literally gave us instructions to 'do nothing, nothing at all, without their written approval or consent,' or some such shit."

After two laps around the grounds, they decided they'd better call a special meeting of the troops this weekend. Things heating up like this made it necessary to cross into Windsor and meet at Tim Horton's on the Canada side of the river. They needed to be more careful than ever.

Chapter 30

Most of the VRS and ACME staff was unmoved by the big wedding that had been held in September. Instead, everyone was preparing for the favorite holiday, the annual Halloween open house at headquarters. Reed spared no expense in turning the stockroom and shipping dock areas into a family friendly haunted house. Many ACME crew members built sets, posed skeletons, and bloodied walls for Fright Night. One area, especially dark and scary, was for adults only.

Fiona's frightening thoughts were more along the lines of the two new bodies in the marketing department with nothing to do. She and Ebony continued to play-act disdain for one another while inside the walls of VRS headquarters. Meeting at the mall or eating lunch at PF Chang's to touch base made life tolerable. They also continued to hold clandestine meetings with Veronica and sometimes Fran.

On two recent occasions Cruz invited the ladies to his meetings with James at Tim Horton's across the border. The tight-knit gang worked stealthily to shore up the solid evidence they hoped would protect them once they left VRS for safe and secure jobs elsewhere. All six of them had decided that staying through the holidays and cashing in on the New Year's bonus season made sense.

Work seemed to calm down to business as usual by the second week of October, four weeks after adding Go and Flo to the group. The two senior executives paraded around as if they attended meetings a-plenty and wrote scores of memos to keep their underlings on task. They mastered the art of pushing a piece of paper from one desk to another in order to look busy in the eyes of those around them. They stuck close together. Go, with no computer experience, needed Flo for typewritten content.

Fiona and Ebony were getting a kick out of coming up with creative ways to stay out of the marketing department. "We'll be in the stockroom posing as attendees for Fright Night booths," or "we both have meetings in Detroit with parade officials about Thanksgiving festivities." Both excuses seemed to appease their new supervisors. Frankly, they figured Go was glad to not have to see them. She and Flo had their own trouble looking busy during forty hour weeks.

Rumors swirled around the newly formed marketing department of five. No advertisements or promotional campaigns, aside from the traditional sponsorships, had cropped up. The senior marketing ladies kept a silent and united front against anyone who dared to ask what, in fact, they did all day. The new normal was simply to stay out of sight, or out of the building, to avoid inquiry.

Fran wrote press releases every now and again with the holiday information. Ebony organized and planned the couple of upcoming events. Fiona tinkered with a Twitter account, perusing social media for alternative energy buzz. Bored, she eventually created and suggested more graphic projects to Jed Jennerson, still just a team of one in Environmental.

She remembered when she'd first met him. He, always inclusive, got along well with everyone. At first, she considered him another non-essential. The tree-hugging MSU grad with a terrific personality did like to include her on his projects, however. As he continued to welcome her on small graphic projects, she began to consider him a Godsend. He was plenty busy, and appreciative of the extra set of hands on whatever odd jobs he had.

Jed was passionate about the environment. "There will be wildlife habitats that engage participation with the community. Here, take a look at this." He drew her attention to the map he'd designed to show her the most recent habitat.

"A zoo?"

"No. Zoos require feeding, maintenance, and security. These will be natural environments where the animals live without help from people. Our interaction with them will be minimal. But to raise an appreciation of nature, we'll conduct guided tours into their terrain."

He welcomed any and all volunteers into his world. He even sent out an inner-office spreadsheet for beer and munchies to encourage sign-ups for a party he planned to host, as thanks for the support.

There was a Michigan versus Michigan State game that would be on television at the shindig, and he added a line to his invite email, "Truc fans only." This meant, don't bring your supervisors.

Ebony, a Michigan State grad, and Fi, from Ann Arbor, prepped betting brackets for wagering. For a $100 buy-in, half the money would be a random pick from the group and the other went toward a random squares page for payouts during the game. Almost everyone had plenty of disposable income working for VRS or ACME. The group of young people who gathered and trusted each other not to rat were always coming up with wagers and bets on random events.

Ebony, navigating a potential move-out from Ben, who hadn't quite left after all, was especially eager for a win. The prize would be a solid two grand.

Fi felt Eb's pressure rising up to the surface. She did her best to reassure her that she could view a split as a very happy occasion.

No need to fret.

The two of them were alone in his kitchen. Attendance at the party for a bit of lighthearted fun.

Although Fiona's experience was with divorce, not kicking out a guy who'd overstayed his welcome, she still understood. Her second husband had conned more than $180,000 out of her. She maintained a sunny disposition throughout the process, but money was always an issue for a single parent.

They debated on Friday whether or not Ebony would attend the party Saturday. "No one can take away your spirit unless you crumble," she told her friend. "Stand tall; take it like a man; pay the bastard off, and move on to something better." They'd grown quite close the past few months. "Lemons into lemonade, remember?"

First to arrive at Jed's place on Saturday, Fi starting unpacking her party contributions.

"Help me understand something, Fiona."

"Yes?"

"Your title is Senior Social Media Specialist, but we're not engaging in anything that's internet communication related. Why is that?"

"Golly, I was sure your email said, 'no work talk' during extra-curricular outings." She wanted to dodge the subject. She knew Jed was counting on the environmental department getting an interactive component launched. He wanted citizens to contact VRS directly with any greenway over-growth or corridor concerns. "I brought homemade ceviche," she added, hoping to change the subject.

"Seriously though, I thought you had Reed wrapped around your finger. You marry off his favorite daughter to a millionaire, post up the invites and all the party favors as your 'wedding gift' and all." Jed was someone Fi had confided in early on. While she trusted him, she certainly had no intention of updating him on the latest findings.

"Yes, Reed is pumped about Vic marrying Kyle, someone to help manage the family finances. But that certainly doesn't translate into my directing marketing strategy under the new regime."

"Oh, right, that. Where the eff did those two old bags come from anyway?" Jed was referring to Go and Flo of course, but she wasn't going to bite.

"Both of those 'old bags' you're referring to came highly recommended by Governor Schneider's boy. You'd be smart to stay on their good side. Just saying."

She watched his expression to make sure he took her seriously.

"Have you got a tray for the crackers? Even a paper plate will do." She needed him to stop asking questions; her self-control only stretched so far.

Jed handed her a large plastic tray just as she saw Fran pass by the kitchen window. "Fran's here, why don't you get the door?"

"I'll arrange the crackers while you get the door. Move out. I want to get the Fireball shots cued up." *Enough VRS talk.*

"You're doing fine," Jed said as he opened the door. "Fran, M' Lady." He kissed her fingertips in a mock medieval greeting. "Come on in." Jed busied himself greeting the next batch of guests. *Bullet dodged,* thought Fiona.

Jed had invited a few pals from his neighborhood, as well as a couple of college buddies. Thankfully, the place filled up with non-VRS folks. Fiona began breathing more comfortably.

When Ebony pulled up to unload a box, Fi trotted out to offer a hand.

"Thanks, Fiona." She sounded out of breath. "Take this in, will ya? I can't stay." Ebony's voice held an edge.

"But the game doesn't start for another hour. Can't you get whatever done and…?"

"I said I can't stay. Butt out. Tell Jed I'm sorry."

Ebony was already pulling her seatbelt back on when Fiona noticed the red swollen eyes behind shaded glasses.

"You okay, Ebony?" Although bummed to be left here alone, she was more concerned about what had upset Eb. Tears suggested that Ben resurfaced. Again. "I can drop this plate inside and join you for a

Starbucks?" She made it sound like a suggestion to keep from appearing too nosy.

"No, Skyler has a basketball game. Once again Ben wormed his way in, then out again. It was a disaster this morning. I'll catch you up on Monday. Be sure I win that raffle, would ya?"

Fiona stared after her as she drove away. No, something was seriously wrong. Ebony would give her the cleaned-up version on Monday, she was sure.

The party was well attended, and the pot rose to over $25,000. Sadly, Ebony was not a winner.

On Monday, Ebony called in sick.

Chapter 31

Over the past few weeks, Wright had helped Fiona and Ebony vet the new leaders in the department. He uncovered information that outlined how they both had narrowly escaped jail time for their roles in promoting fake cable services, in previous marketing positions.

The trio were seated in a Starbucks booth on a Sunday morning when he explained, "In their depositions, they claimed to have been ignorant of the operations of the company." *Easy enough to believe,* Fiona thought, not impressed with either Go's nor Flo's intelligence.

"Anything else?" Ebony had hoped there would be dirt enough to purge them.

"Get out while you still can," Wright told them, looking strangely worried.

"I will. Right after the holidays." Fiona had her consulting work, holidays were busy and good money to head into the New Year less in need of the VRS paycheck.

"I'd suggest sooner," he said.

When Ebony had departed, and it was just she and Wright, Fiona inquired again. "Anything you can tell me?"

"Just a feeling."

But she was sure there was more. When pressed, he just shook his head. "You know I can't comment on an ongoing investigation, especially when one of the informants is directly involved."

"So I'm an informant?" She tried to make a joke of it.

"From the moment you gave me those maps," he said.

"After the holidays," she repeated with a frown.

That glib statement resulted in their first argument. She didn't need pressure from him, too. *Keep the work at work,* she told him as if she could speak into his mind.

#

Crisp, cool fall mornings meant the bone-chilling winter was just around the corner, which filled Fiona with dread. Just back to her desk, sipping the venti no-foam latte she'd reheated for the second time already, her mind wandered to her girls. Would they remember to pull on an additional sweater layer without her at home to remind them? As she glanced at her computer screen, she noticed it was only 7:48 a.m. She could still catch them on the home phone if she dialed right away. They would be brushing their teeth – *they'd better be* – and heading out the door by 7:55

to make it to school by 8. As she lifted the handset to make the call, a shriek rang out from the next cubicle.

Alarmed, Fiona dropped the phone and instinctively jumped out of her chair. She grabbed for the paper cup in time to prevent an unfortunate latte loss as Ebony launched into a full-on tantrum.

It was just three steps to Ebony's side of the divider wall between them.

"Oh my God, Fiona, oh my freaking God!"

Ebony flailed her hands as if the page had burned her. She jogged in place, sobbed and squealed at the same time.

Fiona snatched the note from the floor and read it.

Raised Catholic, Fiona could not shake the repulsion she felt after she read the note. Sure, it had been addressed to Ebony, but the sheer hatred churned out onto the page sent a shiver down Fiona's spine that stayed with her like a terminal illness.

She shuttered her eyes in a feeble attempt to un-see it.

The power of these words.

Egregious headlines about discrimination filled news stories daily; the direct hit to Fiona was primeval. A powerful foreign combination of anger, fear, humiliation, panic, and anxiety rendered her speechless.

A few folks from the accounting department rounded the corner to have a look. Fiona saw tears in the eyes of her coworker.

As quickly as she'd tossed the note, she bent over, snatched it up off the floor, and instructed Fiona, "Follow me!"

They arrived at the central bank of elevators in a matter of seconds. Ebony banged on the up button, shoveling the letter toward Fiona.

As she read the words again, Fiona's eyes filled with tears. Her body began a physical transformation from the stress, fear, hatred, and anxiety that flooded her. Maybe she should have taken Wright more seriously. Her knees began to give way, and she stooped to a squatting position in the cart.

"Oh my God, Ebony! Who sent this?"

"Bitch, we're about to find out!" Ebony moved from fear and tears in one minute to red-hot rage the next. "I've had enough. We're taking this straight to Reed. He *will* take care of it."

Fiona resisted the urge to ask the obvious: *what is Reed going to do for us*? Instead, she kept her mouth shut. Another second into the ride up, their eyes met, Ebony slid down to a seat on the floor with Fiona, and they both began crying.

Jennifer, Reed's personal assistant, saw them in that state as they pulled themselves up and exited the elevator on five.

In spite of her tears, Ebony strode to the oak desk with conviction and dropped the letter on the calendar blotter in front of Jennifer. She snatched three tissues from a box on the desk with her right hand, while guiding Fiona by the elbow with her left. "In here."

Her tone brooked no argument. Fiona let herself be led.

"Reed *will* get to the bottom of this."

How can you be sure? Fiona wanted to ask. *How can you be so freaking sure?*

Ebony pulled Fiona out of elevator with great force. It took her a moment to absorb the magnitude of the situation. Her visceral fear of Reed Jacob was almost more potent than the punch in the gut from the note she'd just read.

Fiona allowed herself to be led. Anxiety overwhelmed her. *This is what an out of body experience is.* Her mind roiled at the thought of confronting her boss. When she pulled against Ebony's firm grip, the woman refused to let go. Fiona didn't know what to think of Reed, but the words "penthouse suite" and "ultimate authority" echoed in her head, filling her with unexplainable fear and fogging her ability to think. A tear slid down her cheek. Her stomach clenched.

She watched Ebony flash a plastic card across the face of the interior wall. The penthouse floor containing Reed Jacob's executive offices was inaccessible without security clearance.

Following two steps behind, Fiona hazily heard a loud and angry Ebony explain to his assistant, Jennifer, the need to interrupt whatever meeting Reed might be in. "This shit just came addressed to me and her." Ebony dropped the paper on to the large oak desk with a huff. "Don't touch it! We're gonna get the fingerprints off that thing and put someone's sorry ass in jail for this!" Ebony's ability to move from fear to fury was impressive.

Nausea overcame Fiona. Grabbing for a pristine leather-wrapped trash bin, she sat down on the first available chair and hugged the receptacle just below her chin. Her mind and body refused to function with so much going on in the room.

In her experience, flying under the radar had always worked. Now, one terrible note had thrust her front and center.

"Ohmygoodness," The unexpected visitors and the out of the blue directive from Ebony alarmed Jennifer. "Should I call 911?" The words fell into empty space as Ebony was already yanking on the door to Reed's office. "He's not. It's locked. I don't. Ohmygoodness."

Clearly, Jennifer was reading the words on the note as she tried to process the situation. After another millisecond and two more "ohmys," Jennifer grabbed a set of keys from a top desk drawer. "Here, let me unlock that for you. You two girls stay right in here while I call security."

Ebony stormed into the office and immediately took to Reed's large leather chair behind the desk. "You call security. I'm calling the police!"

Jennifer did her best to assist Fiona out of the reception area and on to a couch in Reed's office. She was careful not to dislodge the trash can, as she was fully aware of how a mess of vomit on the executive carpet would add an entirely new dimension to the chaos.

Just as Jennifer returned to her desk to call security, the elevator dinged, announcing another arrival. Anxiously, she watched as the door opened. Reed appeared like a Greek God from the back center of the elevator, striding confidently toward her with a bright smile. "Good morning, Sunshine.

Laying open on Jennifer's desk was the note. Reed stood tall and evaluated the piece of paper from a foot away. "Get Security on this, post haste." He stood still another minute as his eyes passed over the note once more. "Jennifer, get Monroe. Immediately.

And whatever you do, do not touch that thing." He strode into his office.

As Jennifer read the note for a third time, tears flowed down her cheeks and dropped on the walnut desk. Quickly swiping a Kleenex from her credenza, she made sure not to wet the thing.

On a plain white sheet of paper were the words:

YOU MAKE OUR GROUP LOOK BAD. WE DON'T LIKE YOUR KIND AT VRS!!!! REED SAID THIS COMPANY IS FOR GOD-LOVING AMERICANS. YOU AND THAT FREAK FIONA ARE ALWAYS CAUSING TROUBLE FOR US. GO BACK TO THE GHETTO AND TAKE YOUR SKINNY N-LOVIN JEW GIRLFRIEND WITH YOU.

Mentally exhausted and settled into her leather chair, she let loose all the stress pent up over her five years with Reed. The secrecy, unlimited expenditures, rendezvous outings; none of that compared with this.

#

Fiona and Ebony spent the rest of the day in conference rooms with Reed, Randy from corporate security, and the local police. Finally, in the late afternoon, the group voted to bring in the Detroit area FBI representative. Because the letter had been mailed to headquarters via USPS, it warranted federal involvement.

Each division asked many of the same questions: "Do you Ebony, or you Fiona, know anyone who would wish you harm?" "Have you had any disagreements with other employees over the past few months?" "Is there any reason for us to believe maybe one of you two, in fact, wrote this letter in order to get out of a work obligation of some kind?"

Fiona leaned into Ebony with "Horse shit! As if you or I could, in a million years, spew that."

The message of hate, and suggestion that she and Ebony were the ones causing trouble, reopened wounds long suppressed by Fiona from the last corporate job she'd held. In her early twenties, she'd worked among a group of "good old boys" at an oil company, surrounded by provocation in many forms.

Her former colleagues complained that she tried to make her male counterparts look bad by suggesting accountability and audits. She endured sexual innuendos verbalized during both pregnancies. They capped off her work experience with three exit interviews after she announced her intention to leave before her ten-year anniversary with the company. "Who in their right mind leaves a well-paying job and company car just months before being fully vested?" they'd asked.

A woman who values her sanity. Now she felt that sanity being threatened again.

The end of the oil company stint resulted in her surviving the past ten years on contract work as a marketing consultant. Self-employment allowed her to steer clear of any projects or people she didn't gel with. She managed to avoid people who refused to appreciate her expertise and guidance in strategizing their businesses.

Until now. This too-good-to-be-true opportunity to join VRS as a digital marketing specialist earned her a hefty salary and secured amazing benefits for her and her two daughters. Just six months ago, they had offered her the newly created position, which she guardedly accepted.

Fiona kept her two part-time employees and the marketing company alive, partly because she'd been with some of her clients for more than a decade. They were like family to her. Perhaps the real reason she kept her company alive was as a safeguard should she be unable to handle the new responsibilities.

Fiona did her best to ignore the jabs and sideways glances from many folks at the firm. So what if they had created a job especially for her? What did they know? In the long run, she was providing the best for her girls, right?

But after ten years of raising two daughters on a bare-bones budget, Fiona realized she was in no position to quit at this time.

Five hours later, Fiona returned to Ebony's cubicle. There it was, lying face up in the bin of discarded mail. Using a Kleenex, she lifted the envelope from the trash and slipped it into her purse.

The local police might "lose" the original letter. She'd get this to Wright. How no one thought of the envelope was not her concern, getting it out in safe condition was. She imagined him using it to get a fingerprint, identify its origin, something.

At her desk, she used a large manila envelope to protect the standard #10. She worked quickly to pack up her laptop and closed the letter safely in its fold. Fiona exited the building unapproached, heart pounding. Sweat pooled atop her forehead, and below her armpits, fortitude was taxing business.

Fiona made her way out to the parking garage, still in a daze. Once she'd located her CRV, her fingers fumbled through the simple act of unlocking the car. Finding the ignition to start the thing proved just as difficult. Fatigue engulfed her. Mind abuzz, she rolled toward the guard gate to exit the expansive VRS grounds, tears began to impede her vision.

She pulled into a nearby gas station to pluck a napkin from the glove box and dry her face. *Deep breaths, Fiona.* More tears followed, requiring another napkin. *Calgon, take me away.* She laughed at her own zany thoughts, but was determined to get on the road before the masses. Reed had dismissed her and Ebony at about three o'clock, and it was nearly four already. *Come on Fi, pull it together.*

Somehow, she managed to get on the freeway headed south toward home, but her mind drifted in and out of awareness, causing a *how did I get here* feeling, both figuratively and literally. She transferred from US 275 to M14. *What the hell am I going to do with myself?*

HONNKK! A loud horn alerted her that she'd crossed the white line and nearly sideswiped the car next to her. *First things first. Watch the freaking road, Fiona.* The horn honk was followed by an aggressive finger from the Chevy driver as he blew past.

Moments later, she caught herself drifting into the rumble strips on the side of the road as her mind wandered through memories of surviving stalkers, death threats, and other crazies in the past.

Just recently, there had been kooky callers after an ad in the yellow pages featured her company's name and phone number. She had never placed an ad for her own services, preferring only to work with clients she'd acquired from referrals. The folks at the *Big Yellow Book* offered no valid explanation for how the ad got in there. However, they eagerly offered her "a renewal of the advertisement at a discounted rate, should she care to sign a contract."

Fiona exited the freeway nearest her home, and arrived safely in her own driveway. The girls would be home any minute. She needed to get herself under control enough to talk calmly with them about what had transpired. Police at VRS headquarters suggested the note was likely just some prankster looking to get a rise out of her and Ebony. "To be on the safe side," the officer had concluded, "be sure to check your tires before leaving the parking lot though, just in case." Were her children in danger now, too?

The FBI representative had really put fear in her and Ebony with his comment about more to come. "Potentially, there will be more memos coming, so be sure to check your home mailboxes and contact me right away if you receive any suspicious mail or packages."

As soon as the garage door rose to the top, Fiona saw her neighbor Kay approaching from across the driveway. Just the sight of Kay, with her sunny smile and obvious offering of food in foil casserole pans, started Fiona crying again. The well-meaning retiree was simply trying to be a good neighbor.

The flow of tears continued as she thanked Kay for the frozen lasagna and closed the door in her face without justification. She managed to turn on the oven and the TV before slouching to the floor in the kitchen, arms clasped around her knees. She simply wanted to give up. More tears soaked her silk blouse with salty water splotches.

What now? Tell the girls she'd had another bad day at the office? The note described Fiona as a skinny Jewish something or other. *Whatever you do, Fiona, do not say the N word in front of the kids. Keep it together. No tears, no dramatic display. The children will mimic your behavior.*

# # #

When Ebony returned to her cubicle, she found Ben waiting. He rushed to her and took her in his arms.

She let him hold her for a while, relishing the comfort.

As they broke apart, she looked around. "Where's Skyler?"

"Oh, I found a babysitter for him. I thought..."

"You thought what? You thought that the reason you don't have a job, or an income from that business you were supposed to start up, or even help with the groceries, or paying for that babysitter is on me somehow?"

"Look, baby…" He tried to get close for another hug.

She shoved him away. Suddenly it all made sense. Everything about Ben was a sham, even that comforting hug. There was nothing real about him. He was a plastic man. All this time she thought he was real, or at least a part of him was. But as she looked in his eyes, she realized he only thought about himself. That hug wasn't out of love, or even compassion. It was so she would continue to think he cared.

But this latest incident at VRS had shown her something. It was a sham, too. Just like Ben's beautiful brown eyes, VRS only cared for itself. It was time to take charge, and stop being the victim of everything that looked good on the outside.

She took Ben's arm. "Let me help you out of the building. Let me help you to my car. And let me help you pack. You're leaving right now, 'baby.' My life is changing for the better, and it's better without you."

"But I just moved back in. It'll take me days to find everything again…"

"Oh, don't worry about your things. They'll be out on the lawn. You can pick them up at your leisure."

"Can't we talk about this over dinner?"

She laughed. "Tell you what. While you enjoy your dinner alone, you talk about it. That's what you do best, isn't it? Talk? That's the only real thing about you."

Chapter 32

Wednesday morning Fiona awoke from a nightmare. She couldn't shake the feeling of impending doom.

In the dream she swam toward a shore that she never reached. While she heard a group of people laughing, no one tried to rescue her. Instead, their partying got louder. Her limbs refused to continue their strokes and kicks. The partying increased in volume even as her limbs refused to cooperate.

The next moment she found herself in a dark stairwell, making every attempt to move. But her body still refused to function. As she coughed up water from her lungs, a "bad guy" rushed past her down the stairs. For some reason he never saw her. Somehow she melted into the concrete wall for safety.

When she awoke, she tried to settle her breathing. She reached for the notebook on her bedside table. Keeping a few notes about her nightmares was an idea from her childhood when they assailed her almost nightly for a time.

She remembered when she had first decided to record them. The great argument between her parents had awakened her. Her mother, finally, decided to move away from their abusive relationship.

But the plan was short-lived. Mom found herself pregnant with her fourth child and decided to stay. Fiona cried that night. Afterward the worst of the nightmares began.

The nightmares returned full force when her high school beau announced (why did he need to *announce* it?) that they'd be having sex for the first time. Why couldn't he just love her?

The nighttime horror shows always occurred when she felt the most vulnerable.

"Eventually the nightmares go away," a friend told her once. Well, they had lessened, anyway. Now she rarely needed to record more than a single entry in a week's time.

But as she poised the pen to write down the horrible dream, most of it had already slipped away. All that she scribbled was, "I'm afraid I will drown" and "I was invisible. The bad guy couldn't get me." *Just three lines. Damn it!*

Writing them down, though, reminded her how much she felt her life spinning out of her control. This had been the third nightmare this week. *No, it makes sense. I'm in danger. Before, I believed it might be so, but now the note.* Her instinctive feeling had become a reality.

A glance at the clock forced another curse. *Four in the morning, too late to get back to sleep, with less than seven hours of sleep to manage through yet another stressful day.*

Fiona knew sleep deprivation added to the stress. She wondered if Wright hadn't given her good advice about leaving VRS immediately. She was beginning to doubt she could hold on long enough to get the holiday bonus in January.

She took the stairs as quietly as possible so as not to wake the girls and fired up the HP in the kitchen. Logging in to the VRS company hub, she quickly responded to a couple of emails, then typed out a SICK DAY email to Go and Flo.

According to their new policy, any electronic communication to Go must also be copied to Flo. The gang all knew the real reason. Go could barely fire up a computer much less check email or formulate replies. The woman had zero computer skills. No ability to schedule on Microsoft Outlook, she had to dictate memos to Flo for circulation. Fi considered her a useless dinosaur of a human being, employed simply to drive up the bottom line "marketing expenses of VRS." Diabolical and ridiculous, she knew, but straight truth.

Fi sent a separate email from her personal Gmail account to let Ebony know she wouldn't be in, but that she was available if she or anyone else needed anything.

She climbed back into bed just before the clock registered five. As she placed her head on the pillow, she reminded herself three times to disarm the alarm that would soon shake her awake. So much cluttered her head, she was positive she'd be unable to get back to sleep.

At seven, Allison shook her awake. "Mom, you slept through your alarm. You're going to be late and this time it isn't on us."

Fiona, dazed and confused for a second, broke into laughter. When she saw the confused look on her daughter's face, she laughed even harder. "You are going to be such a good mom, Ali."

Chapter 33

Thursday morning, half-past seven, Wright Danielson parked his old Chevy on Elm Street, about a block from Ebony's home. Fiona hadn't asked him to, and Newtown was out of his jurisdiction, but it was his day off, and he hoped to make points with Fiona to make up for their recent argument. A little surveillance might do exactly that.

So from his "clunker" (only on the outside; the inside ran like a dream), he kept his eye on the small red brick ranch. He'd heard Ebony had kicked Ben out. He wanted to make sure.

Where he parked offered him a clear view of her place on the south side of the street. At ten to eight the garage door rose. Danielson took pictures of a tall black man exiting the front door of the home with a bag of trash, as if a chore or two would let him back in Ebony's life.

Wait, what? Wright watched the guy look toward the front to be sure no one was looking. He popped the trunk of a rusted-out Oldsmobile on the street and tossed the bag in quickly. As he passed the garage again, he grabbed the trash receptacle and pulled it to the curb, as if that was his reason for being there.

Well, well, well. Benny, my boy, you saving something for later? Wright took down the license plate and called it in to the station nearest Ebony's home.

"Concerned citizen here. I think you've got a possible burglary. Maybe not, but I saw this guy come out of a home with a bag of trash. I paid it no mind until I watched him put the bag in the trunk of his car. Might be nothing, but I thought you should know. He was acting odd about the barrel he later pulled to the curb, just looked to me like a theft as opposed to a favor." He gave the dispatcher the plate number and cross streets he watched Ben exit on.

"Your name, sir?" The clerk sounded appreciative.

Wright gave a fake name. He had blocked his phone number prior to calling. "It's almost bus time, ma'am. Oh, my! Is he drunk? He jumped a curb and ran a stop sign. You ought to send someone quick before something drastic happens." He hung up before she could inquire further.

Wright drove around the next block and parked across from Dunkin' Donuts.

A while back, Ebony told Fiona she suspected that Ben simply waited at the local donut shop for her and Skyler to leave, then hot-footed back in to sit on her couch all day, watching the tube.

Not today, pal. We're going to have a look in that trunk of yours, aren't we?

The local police usually responded to incidents in quiet neighborhoods like this within minutes.

Right on cue, as the Olds turned onto the main drag, lights began flashing.

To Danielson's delight, Ben pulled into the Dunkin' Donuts lot. He'd pop over under the guise of offering help. Wright left his car and crossed the street.

"Step out of the car, sir," the officer told Ben.

Wright noticed that the officer's knuckles were white. He appeared nervous and out of his league.

Wright stepped onto the scene and showed his badge. "Well, morning, officer. Routine call-out?"

"Reported 4200. I already called for backup." He turned back to Ben. "I asked you to step out of the vehicle, sir. What part of that did you not understand?"

He seemed more confident now that Wright was within range, should anything go astray.

"Yeah. Well, I was looking for my registration, dude. What are you pulling me over for?" Ben seemed discombobulated, but showed no move to obey the officer.

"I said out of the car." The officer became more forceful as another patrol car zipped next to them from the back of the building. As Ben rose from the vehicle, the officer demanded, "Hands on the hood. Now."

Ben complied.

"You have the right to remain silent," the officer said.

"What the fuck?" Ben moved as if to return to his car when he saw two additional uniforms headed his way. "I didn't do shit. You got no right."

The local police paused. One took out his breathalyzer kit, but he hesitated as if he wasn't sure he should. Ben didn't appear to be drunk.

Wright headed around to the back of the vehicle, as if he saw something. "Officer, maybe we should check out the vehicle. Check for any drugs or alcohol. Pop the trunk even."

"We've got this, sir. Who are you?" One of the newly arrived officers confronted him.

Wright slapped the wallet open to his detective ID and badge. "Just happened to be in the neighborhood, pal, no biggie." He backed up a step or two and waited while one officer checked the glove box from the passenger side and another popped the lever releasing the trunk from the driver's side.

Danielson watched in satisfaction while one officer assured Ben that he would be heading downtown to explain the marijuana in the center console, and the CPU packed as if it was trash in the trunk.

Wright snapped a few shots of the trunk and an officer as he held up the marijuana bag before he left.

He found all the confirmation he needed to run a background on Ben.

When he returned to his car, he texted Fiona. "Ask Ebony if she still has her home computer. CMM." That was their text code for "call me maybe, it's not urgent."

Fiona responded right away, "Will do. E not here yet. Staff meeting in ten, CYL ASAP." Then a second text, "thanks." *CYL, call you later,* Wright noted. *Soon, I hope.*

By her thanking him he felt relieved. At least she was listening to him.

Chapter 34

Preparing for the VRS sponsored pancake breakfast the day before the annual Thanksgiving Day Parade, Cruz, James, Fiona, Ebony, and Veronica circled around an eight-seat table with coffee and donuts. Cruz and James, celebrity chefs, always impressed the ladies when they offered their support for various volunteer roles.

VRS intended to sponsor the actual parade along with Macy's in years to come. The parade was one of Reed's favorite events. Dressed as a clown for the tenth year in a row, he was funny and charming. It was easy to follow the public face of Reed Jacob. His group from the country club, all CEOs and presidents of this or that in the Detroit area, joined him in both costumes and camaraderie each year.

James was obviously anxious about something. He began a long diatribe about how this group, right here at this table, possessed the ability to truly *be something*. "If we stick together as part of a community service like this, we're reminded that not only are we assisting a select group in this effort, and we are serving the greater good." He continued on with "we are creating a better world, and can rest assured that help will be there for us as well, when needs arise. As we offer our own light to a collective good side in a time of darkness, all of our lights will become brighter."

Cruz spoke next. "I think the light James is referring to is symbolic. We all know about the letter Ebony received, and how all of us feel about the changes being blanketed over us at headquarters. We need to be making some rather large decisions soon. Fish or cut bait. Sink or swim. Speak or conceal."

James jumped in. "Veronica, we're thrilled about your position at your father's firm. To tell you the truth, I'm glad you're safely out of this mess."

"That doesn't mean I don't care. Ebony and Fiona have kept me up to date, so please continue. I'm your cheering section."

"We're all feeling exactly the same way, James." Ebony stood. "But now is not the time nor the place for this." She motioned her head to the hundreds of other people surrounding them in the tent.

"Kinda might be." Fiona spoke quietly. "No audiovisual recording devices, a casual donut and coffee with purpose. If we get caught meeting like this, it could be damning. Detective Danielson has offered us police protection, but we all know that won't be effective. They want us gone, Ebony, one way or another."

All but Fiona were financially vested, to the tune of millions of dollars. All eggs in one basket. The VRS and ACME Company's success directly related to their financial freedoms.

###

A commotion at midpoint in the parade made local news. Four suited men approached one of the clowns and escorted him from the festivities. Rumor had it, Reed Jacob was the white-faced, red-nosed performer. He left without incident and on-lookers paid very little attention.

Reed's son-in-law, Kyle, in his first appearance as a parade clown, exited quickly through the thick crowd on the opposite side of the street.

Chapter 35

Wright was hesitant to be in the room with this group. Thanksgiving Day he should be at work in Ann Arbor making double time, but it had been his tip to FBI that warranted this meeting.

An attorney for Reed Jacob, Leonard Mancioni, sat opposite him. Everyone in his own armchair at the London Chop House downtown. The attorney glared at him, wanting answers. Despite the tension and air of crisis, Reed was jovial in his demeanor.

"Clowning here or there matters none to me. I swear it was the coldest day in the history of the damned parade. You all swooped in to save frostbite."

"Reed, no talking, remember?" The attorney spoke the words while staring at Wright. "Which one of you is responsible for interrupting my client this morning?" The attorney's tone was accusatory, eyes on Wright.

"Here's what we've got," began one of the agents. "We find ourselves in a challenging situation with multiple reports from several sources."

"Bullshit." Reed's attorney rose. "Challenge with a search warrant, or you'll be out of jobs. All of you. Reed, let's go."

On a sudden inspiration, Wright stood and dropped an electronic device on the table. "I took the liberty of making you a copy, Sir." Contempt in his eyes, he held Reed's glare. "It's the beginning of the end."

Reed was shoveled out of the room before he could reply. Wright slid back into his chair and let out an audible sigh. He grimaced.

"Calm down, Detective. We rattled him. That's all for today gentlemen. Let's eat." The agent waved for a server. The group dined on turkey and traditional fixings.

Wright moved the food around his plate for half an hour before he excused himself to the restroom. He left out the back door.

Chapter 36

Reed, Ebony, and Jennifer were gathered in the executive conference room to work out the details for a photo booth and other particulars of the upcoming annual Christmas party. Ebony knew Reed trusted her, or at least she thought he did. Not a word was spoken in regard to the parade interruption.

In the past couple weeks, Reed had mentioned several times, however, how he wished he hadn't hired that ridiculous Fiona. He had said things like "if she hadn't been Vic's pal," he would have dismissed her long before now. But Victoria had insisted. One person he couldn't say no to was his beautiful daughter Victoria.

Today, Ebony got the feeling he was sounding her out. Jennifer exited to grab a phone call at her desk, leaving the two of them alone.

"So, Eb, you all straight after that silly note you got?"

He's working so hard to keep it casual.

"Depends, boss. Some days I think I'm okay, and then someone drops a book on the floor and my heart rate shoots through the roof. Not sleeping. Skyler hears me cry in the night. I can't eat. I look over my shoulder in the Kroger checkout line. Straight is not a word I would go with. Twisted maybe. Twisted AF."

"AF?" Reed eyed her with genuine curiosity.

"Twisted as fuck. S'cuse my French, Reed. Imagine you're surrounded by a bunch of black women on an island where you're the only white man in sight. Straight? Nah, I think you'd be pretty darned twisted up deciding who you could trust. Am I right?"

"Aw, come on now, Eb. Don't get my imagination stirred up like that. That's one of my favorite daydream scenarios, Sugar. Deserted island. Nothing but dark chocolate for miles."

"You're an ass, Reed." Ebony, having years of experience with his male chauvinism, still never failed to find herself feeding his vivid imagination.

Jennifer returned to save further off-color comments. "Okay, you two. One photo booth or two this year? Last year we had a geo-tag with VRS in one, ACME in the other. Same same?"

"Same." Ebony

"Same," Reed said at the exact moment Ebony did.

"Jinx," she said.

He smiled at her. He never took his harassment too far with Ebony. She believed he genuinely cared about her and Skyler.

"Eb, you want me to assign you one of my guys over the holiday? Are you seriously worried that something else will happen?" Reed could be a decent man some days.

"Thanks, but we're heading to my mom's place in Houston. I need a change of scenery."

"Well, that sounds perfect, kiddo. You want the company plane for the trip?"

"Booked on Delta, sir. Thank you, though." Ebony needed to let go of all the corporate perks and whatnot when she left.

"Yoo-hoo," Jennifer interrupted again. "Party planning, folks. This holiday party is not going to plan itself."

"We trust you, Jennifer," Reed offered.

"Whatever you think, Jennifer," Ebony said at the same time. When she stood up to leave, Reed pulled her in for an awkward embrace.

"Anything. Anything at all, just call me," Reed whispered in her ear.

Ew Ew Ew thought Ebony. Fiona was right. These guys are super creepy. She left without another word.

Chapter 37

The Redd Foxx restaurant in Bloomington was packed with patrons celebrating the holidays. Reed and his posse dined near the back at their regular table. No lady friends in tow.

Missing from the group of usual suspects was Larry Monroe, former head of security detail, who had been charged and found guilty of first-degree murder in the death of Muller, manslaughter in the case of Fitzgerald.

Feds came in through the kitchen, made a stealth removal of Reed, barely a silverware drop of commotion. Four of the five fellows at the table barely raised their heads as witness.

###

Tulie greeted guests at the VRS annual Christmas party later that night. Her very contagious husband hated to miss out on the festivities.

"Reed so wishes he could be here with you all. Every one of you in this room is like family to us. He might like it if you all were to toss back a Fireball shot in his honor. Bartender, cue them up!" She went on about how he'd picked up a virus in the late hours before the party, but no one could hear her over the loud cheer, "Fireball." The popular Pitbull song by the same name blasted over the sound system, and the dance floor erupted.

###

Two days later at the arraignment, a lengthy list of indictments was read. Federal prosecutors likened the case to a master conspiracy led by Reed Jacob and promised more criminals and charges would follow. There were charges ranging from failing to file proper notifications in service matters, to solicitation and conspiracy to commit murder. Jacob as the kingpin, dozens of potential conspirators remained in queue.

When the judge ordered Jacob held without bond, the courtroom erupted with whispers and murmurs. Reed was handcuffed and led out the side door without even a glance toward his wife in the front row.

Light bulbs flashed, reporters sped through exit doors to waiting camera crews crowded in front of the courthouse.

"Order. Order in the court." Mayhem overruled his words as folks pushed and shoved past bailiffs.

Chapter 38

Detective Danielson arranged to meet Ebony at Starbucks and brought photos.

"Ben is cheating."

"I knew it!"

"Bet you don't know this. He and Reed Jacob meet for drinks. Often."

Ebony turned a shade of gray.

"They meet at the Oilman's Club with a radio guy named JT Morton. Although they're not on the same team, they bowl in a league together. Then they happen upon one another afterward for beers, they and another fellow, former FBI agent and head of security, Larry Monroe. If you have read the papers, you know all about him by now."

"Furthermore, we lifted one clear fingerprint off the envelope Fiona brought to us. The one your anonymous note was mailed in. It belongs to Monroe. He's under investigation for a number of additional crimes that I can't divulge right now."

"His hit man. Hell, head of security," Ebony whispered. "I bet he was the one who planted the bug under my car. He knew, every vehicle of each employee there."

"He was. Some of these things will come out at his next trial."

"He's been arrested right? Can he get out and have any further contact with any of us?"

"I hope not. But you need to remain vigilant. Are you prepared to testify against him?"

"I signed a non-disclosure agreement when I was hired on. So did Fiona. We can't testify."

"Then we'll need to depend on the facts we have uncovered. Not only is your ex complicit, but so is a man named Jeff, who we believe pushed Fort into the wet cement hole. The death at the warehouse back in March ties in as well. The unfortunate death before the Fourth of July celebration provided two teeth with the DNA still intact. We have one assailant in custody, as well as the supervisor who tried to cover it up."

"Reed wasn't responsible for that."

"We know. But we have several reports of him arriving on the site and congratulating the men for their quick thinking."

"Thank you," she said. "You didn't need to get rid of Ben for me, but it helps."

"So what will you do with your life? Are you planning to leave VRS?"

"I already have. I start my teaching practicum on Monday."

"Good for you."

"What about Joe's death, do we know what happened?"

"Unfortunately, there's more work to do on that. We can't prove anything, yet. The bugs I planted didn't relay any valuable information. And that coil I suspected to be of Russian manufacture basically disappeared."

"At least I have my life back. You know what I really want to do more than teach? I want to counsel young women on life choices. We don't, any of us, need to get stuck with a Ben because of deep brown eyes and incredible charm. We need to be faithful to our goals, and if our prospective partner doesn't get it, then he gets the door."

#

Fiona congratulated herself on making it through the holidays. To be sure she would still get her bonus, she hired a law firm to look over the severance package. Everything was in order.

She sighed in relief. *Even though I still have nightmares, at least I'm doing all right financially.*

"You were wrong," she told Wright as they snuggled together on the sofa.

"Wrong about what?" He flipped the channel changer a dozen times, looking for something he wanted to watch.

"Wrong about me needing to leave VRS early."

"I wasn't wrong. You were just lucky. We arrested Larry Monroe before he carried out the hit on you."

"Hit!?" she croaked.

"Don't worry. He'll be in prison a long time."

Chapter 39

Fourteen hundred miles south of Detroit, James was relieved that Reed was finally behind bars. He read about it from the chaise lounge, poolside, in Naples, Florida. Sad. Relieved. Happy. Miserable. All at the same time. His wife Jeannie pulled her chair closer and put her hand on his.

Life is good.

# # #

Reed Jacob was removed from the courtroom and processed through intake. The crew at the local jail strip searched and examined him for any exceptional medical issue, oblivious that this inmate was any different from the next. The ice cold shower and jumpsuit infuriated him.

From his twelve-by-twelve cell, Reed Jacob wondered how long it would be before he would slowly lose his mind in here. Less than seventy-two hours earlier, seated in a conference room just outside of the crowded federal courtroom, his question and answer session with his team of lawyers had been centered on the dismissal of all charges. Payment of their fees, closing out the case, basically their plans for quickly getting him back on track. His lavish lifestyle and reputation restored. Walking in he'd been so confident.

Yet, here he sat, alone and frustrated as hell.

The hearing didn't go well, he finally admitted. The list of people indicted and arrested filled pages of legal tripe. Larry Monroe, arrested on multiple counts. First-degree murder, manslaughter, and tampering to name a few. Jeff what's-his-name indicted for second-degree murder. Most of his upper-level office staff, such as the two marketing executives and Ivan Gregory, all indicted. And those were just the tip of the iceberg. Dozens more fell to the legal system, the same one he had so carefully manipulated his whole life. His youngest son, Scott, whom he had kept out of the business by design, would need to step up to the plate.

To make matters worse, Tulie, the bitch, sued him for divorce. Victoria never visited. Kyle, filthy rich because of what Reed had done for him, never communicated either. He had only Scott, his youngest son, to carry out the plan.

What he had wanted was a well-deserved vacation to the Canary Islands with his children and grandchildren. Yes, Victoria told him she was pregnant but said he'd never get the chance to see the child, either in this life or the next. How could she so completely turn on him like that?

Then he had to endure all that horse-shit about securities fraud and illegal limited liability partnerships and operations. His attorneys had assured him all of the legal filings were simply preliminary findings, trumped-up charges, in fact. If so, what was he doing here?

I need to get new attorneys.

Reed had spoken to his DC associates and lawyers just last week about how they were cooperating with authorities, had fully disclosed all details. They assured him they were not, and had not, violated any rules. On the off chance that any charges were to land on solid ground, the group would immediately file bankruptcy examinations, some chapter something, to stave off the hounds at the Department of Justice. Hell, no one had gone to jail after the Enron situation. Or had they? Reed needed at least his cell phone and a legal pad to make notes.

Nothing was getting done right. He should be on vacation, not wallowing here. The feds had their man, or men, rounded up over the killings. No blood on his hands.

Reed was deep in thought about travel details, now flummoxed by this "temporary incarceration." *Geez, I hope these guys get me the hell out of here today. With the yacht booked out of Ana Maria Island, sailing to the Keys is now out, we'll have to take the private plane directly to Tenerife.* It was long past time to kick back and celebrate his successes -- enough jabber about this nonsense that he may have skimmed, bribed, killed, snared, or hustled anyone.

There was a clank of keys and an armed guard carried what looked like a three-weeks-old Banquet frozen dinner on a metal tray.

"You'll be transferred to federal prison tomorrow where the food isn't as good. It's your last night here, enjoy it."

Chapter 40

Scott Jacob remained loyal. He didn't read The New York Times, though made a quick daily search each morning for his father's name. He set a Google alert, which occasionally missed VRS or Reed Jacob when the key words were spelled wrong -- Jacobs with an s-- or were buried in the body of an article, as was the case today.

He read the story again, and took a few notes on how much money this reporter believed was being "skimmed" prior to the public offering of the "former MidWest Energy agent Jacob and Associates had potentially embezzled." He quickly noted the name of the journalist and texted his father's legal lead, Mancioni. "Shut it down. NYT Steinman." He was banking on the fact that Mancioni too had seen the piece.

As Scott tipped back in his chair, he wondered about asking his father point-blank about the money trail. He knew he'd never get a straight answer, and over the past few months he had decided he in fact did not want to know the answer. The nagging feeling that the cash-for-fixing scheme might actually be a bogus set up, masterminded by his own father. If anyone could pull off such a massive take, it was his father. But how would they all stay out of jail if some nosey body reporter got too close prior to the sale?

He had questions piling up, elusive answers were causing him sleep loss and itchy trigger fingers. He sent another text to Mancioni. "Time for a magazine?" Magazine in this instance meaning bullets. He would figure something out, but needed more time.

He wondered then about his off shore accounts. Scrolling through his contacts, he texted the "Swiss Cheese Purveyor" via a dark web text account. "Moving day." He typed those two words with sweaty palms. Having vacationed about a year ago in Italy, he was introduced to a trusted Swiss banker willing to facilitate draining all of his US assets for a small fee.

Could he trust this near stranger now that the day had actually arrived? Would his wife Sharon go along with his seemingly impulsive idea of moving to a faraway island, just they and the children? She had guffawed the idea while there. Citing proper schooling, family ties, "a normal childhood," all reasons why he'd married her in the first place she reminded him. Could he risk staying state-side if this thing blows up? He'd hidden in the shadows this long.

ACKNOWLEDGMENTS

You don't always know why a person, project, or player enters your personal energy field, or life, until much later when the blurred lines become clearer. Only then can you see from a distance that the lines in fact were dangerous, even deadly, for some. You jumped a few ropes together, survived a few hard times, and revel in the splendor of a friendship more valuable than any job or paycheck.

This novel is fiction based on a true story where two women were thrown together on a project, threatened, and then discarded. It took years for clarity and ah-ha moments to become this tale. This is one story of the power of women. Loyal, honest, hardworking single mothers, who prevail in spite of the big bad world of liars, cheaters and thieves in their midst.

It would be interesting if folks started investigating utility companies responsible for say, wild fires. When will enough be enough?

ABOUT THE AUTHOR

R Read is new to writing, having self-published two books prior, She Too and Describing Water. Both are available on Amazon and electronically. Check out her books free on Overdrive using your local library affiliation. She has an author page on Amazon and Goodreads. You can message her at R Read Writing on Facebook. She lives in San Luis Obispo, California.

13943724R00149

Made in the USA
San Bernardino, CA
14 December 2018